D0721224

Middle SCHOOL NiNJA: LEGACY

BY MARCUS EMERSON
AND NOAH CHILD

ILLUSTRATED BY DAVID LEE

EMERSON PUBLISHING HOUSE

ALSO BY MARCUS EMERSON

This one's for all you ninjas out there...

"I work for my legacy now
because I won't have time when I'm gone."

- Dr. Ashley Tenderfoot (Feb 2062)

01

Stupid ideas don't seem so stupid when you're about to go through with the stupid idea. *Really* stupid ideas shine brighter the second they enter your brain. Like, "Hey, man, you prob'ly shouldn't do what you're about to do!" I like to think of a field of kittens when that happens… makes it easier to ignore my common sense.

Ahhhhh… field kittens.

My name is Max… and I was about to do something really stupid.

The air smelled of freshly cut grass as birds chirped from trees full of leaves. I took a deep breath as I stalled, hoping a meteor would crash into the planet so I wouldn't have to go through with the thing.

Kids just getting to school lined the sidewalk, curious about what was happening.

I squeezed the handlebars of my bike, listening to the sound of tightening rubber under my fingers.

"Max, you okay?" Beck, my best friend, said from somewhere. I didn't know where exactly since fear was making everything blurry.

I shook my head to clear the fog. "Never been better," I said. "Are… are the thrusters working?"

It took him a second to answer. "I'unno. I never tested 'em."

I nodded bravely like a hero who was about to meet his maker. "Nice."

It became blazingly obvious that the world wasn't going to end anytime over the next few seconds, which meant I was

1

gonna have to perform the stunt that everyone was waiting to see.

The stunt wasn't anything crazy – just a kid jumping his bike over the bike rack filled with other bikes. In front of the bike rack was a cement lip that curved at the bottom, making a nice little ramp that everyone joked about jumping their bike off of.

I was about to be the kid that did it.

Easy enough, right?

Well, my buddy, Beck, thought it'd be epic if I attached some thrusters to the back of my bike. No rocket fuel or flames – just a couple of cans of ultra-compressed air that would fire when I flipped the switch. It was a rig he built himself – that was kind of Beck's specialty.

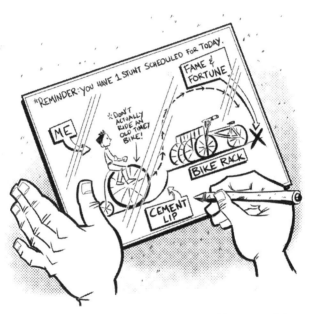

Jumping the rack was a stunt that I'd been working on for weeks. I knew I wanted to do it because of all the kids who *hadn't* done it before.

And I was gonna *nail* it, and the whole school – *no*, the whole school district – *no*... the *whole city* was gonna talk about it when it was done.

"*Did you see that?*" they would say.

"*Oh man, I'm so glad I didn't miss it!*"

"*That was a killer jump, man!*"

Ok, so maybe they wouldn't say *that*, but if anything, jumping the bike rack was at least gonna put me on the map, and I was gonna be the cool kid everyone talked about for, like, a week.

I was a daredevil. I mean, I *wanted* to be one.

The only problem with being a daredevil was that you had to be fearless, and at that moment, sitting on my death-cycle, I was drenched in fear.

So I was kind of a daredevil *wannabe*.

Not poser. *Wannabe*.

"Maybe I shouldn't—" I started to say, but stopped when I saw her.

It was Alexis Miller, but everyone just called her Lexi. Her hair was always tied into two tight ponytails behind her head, and I'm not sure why, but every time I saw her, I thought of strawberries.

Field kittens and strawberries – my happy place.

"Hey, Max!" she said with a hop in her step.

I nodded, head up. "S'up?" I said, cranking the switch as far as it could go on the thruster Beck had attached to my bike. She totally saw me do it. Stud status *confirmed.*

And then I said, "You ready to see some sweet history being made?"

Why did I say that? Who even talked like that? Some sweet history? Ugh! Stud status denied!

"Just don't let this end like last time," she said.

"*Puh-lease*," I said, squeezing the handlebars harder to hide my trembling. "I *got* this!"

Lexi was talking about my last stunt. Let's just say it didn't end the way I wanted it to end. Like, the amount of blood that left my body that day was more than a doctor would recommend.

Unless the doctor was a vampire doctor. Then he prob'ly would've been like, "Oh, man! *This is awesome!*"

WHAT SHOULD'VE HAPPENED

4

WHAT ACTUALLY HAPPENED

Suddenly, Beck spoke loudly, concerned. "Did you just give the thrusters full power?"

My bike shook under me. I raised my eyebrows and did my best to *not* look like a scared little cat, trying to – *scaredy cat! That's* where they got that term!

I tried to sound cool, but my cracking voice made sure I didn't. "You *know* it."

"Turn it back down!" Beck said frantically. "If you give it full power, you'll end up jumping right over the building! There's a ten second timer, so do it fast!"

I had at least eight seconds left.

Quickly, I grabbed the knob on the handlebars and twisted it back to the left. The whole thing snapped off.

"*Eeeep!*" I shrieked.

"It's okay!" Beck said. "Just hit the '*BAIL*' button!"

I looked all over the handlebars for a "*BAIL*" button, but it was nowhere to be found. Following the single wire that led down the frame to the two thrusters by the back tire, I still couldn't find the "*BAIL*" button Beck was talking about.

"*Where's the button?*" I shouted.

Five seconds.

The kids who circled me giggled, pointing their thin fingers at the clown on the bike. They were getting excited because a boring stunt was about to turn into an epic disaster.

"The button should be on the handlebars!" Beck yelled.

I looked again at the handlebars. Except for the broken switch, they were empty. "There's no button!"

Three seconds.

"Oh," Beck said, laughing like a horse. He held a small circular knob in his hand. "It's right here. I forgot to attach it!"

"*Are you serious?*" I screamed.

Zero seconds.

The thrusters behind my feet both went off at the same time with a "*FSHHHHHHH!*" sound. My body jerked back as the bike took off at an irresponsibly high speed. Instinct kicked in, and I squeezed the handlebar grips to keep myself from falling off.

Clenching my teeth, I zoomed past the other students on the sidewalk outside the school. Some were cheering, but to be honest, most were there to see me crash.

The cement lip was coming up fast – way *too* fast. I knew that if I hit it going at that speed, I was gonna find myself on the roof of the school. That, or find myself splattered like a bug on the side of the building.

Did I really have any other choice? I was already on the bike, and it was going fast enough that my eyes were watering.

Plus Lexi was watching! Along with about half the school…

But I didn't want to end up like a splattered bug, so I squeezed my eyes shut and did the only thing I could think of.

I dove off my bike at the last second.

Students jumped out of the way as I rolled across the grass. My book bag tumbled right alongside me, spilling all my junk across the lawn.

Grass always looked so soft and inviting when your face wasn't smashing into it over and over again.

The whole thing only took two seconds, but it felt like an eternity because I could *feel* everyone staring at me. Part of me hoped I'd just keep rolling until I disappeared over a hill or something.

The school's brick wall stopped my escape from the laughing students. Buchanan School was known for having some powerfully sturdy walls. It must've been because most of the building still had the original bricks from two hundred years ago.

My world was spinning even though I had stopped. Upside-down and against the wall, I watched my bike wobble uncontrollably toward the cement lip I was *supposed* to jump. It never made it that far though.

The thrusters were still shooting which made the bike flop around like a fish out of water. It finally crashed into one of the water fountains on the side of the school. The sound of metal crunching against metal was gnarly.

Weeks of work down the drain! Weeks of planning! Of dreaming! Of drawing sketches of me owning the trick! *Gone!*

Every inch of my body burned with pain as I rolled to my butt, but it was the laughter that really stung.

A bunch of kids were pointing their Holo Pens at me, recording video that they'd show their friends later.

"*Did you see that?*" someone said.

"*Oh man, I'm so glad I didn't miss it!*" some girl said.

"*That was a killer jump, man!*" some kid shouted, throwing out a thumbs-up.

Not exactly how I imagined it.

Leaning against the wall, I stayed completely still. I *wasn't* crying, but I knew that if I moved a muscle, I *would've* cried, so… I just sat there.

"Could be worse," I mumbled to myself, trying to keep my spirit high.

At that exact second, a rotten apple splattered on top of my head.

02

Outside the school, like, a minute later.

It didn't take long for everyone to get bored with the kid smeared against the wall. After about a minute, most of the students had found something better to do.

"Ugh," I grunted as I wiped most of the rotten apple out of my hair and off my face. "So gross…"

My book bag was still strewn out across the grass. My tablet and Holo Pen were about five feet away and didn't look damaged. Those things were indestructible. But if a school was gonna hand out hundreds of them to a bunch of sixth graders, I guess they *should* be.

A little farther out from my tablet was a crunched up brown paper sack. That would be the lunch my mom had made for me. She wouldn't be happy to hear that it was destroyed during one of my stunts, but… she didn't need to know.

Someday I was going to be a famous daredevil. Then I'd payback all the things that had to break in order for me to get there. The windshield of my dad's truck. The front door of my house. *Four* bikes. *Seven* skateboards. The entire field behind my house. A fire truck (don't ask). And my grandma's walker (also, don't ask).

Back in the day, there were people who performed stunts *just* to perform stunts. Like, they'd jump a motorcycle over school busses, walk a tightrope between two skyscrapers, parachute into a deep cave, and other crazy things.

And yeah, I might not have been the greatest daredevil who ever lived, but my life wasn't over yet. I still had plenty of time to level up in courage.

Students puddled at the front doors of Buchanan waiting for the bell to ring. I watched as they shuffled their feet to get a few inches closer to the entrance, like zombies who could smell nearby brains.

Groaning, I pushed myself to my feet, not excited about another day of school.

Maybe *school* just wasn't something I was good at. Maybe I was only good at daredevil stunts and—no, nevermind. Not even that. I wasn't really good at *anything*.

But that's exactly why I *needed* to be good at it.

I'd been a sixth grader for a few months now, and I was starting to see that my life *wasn't* the exciting movie that I wished it was. I'd gotten bored and felt more and more let down with each day that passed.

I don't know – it just felt like I was living the same day *every single day*. Like, *nothing* ever changed.

I wake up at seven, ride my bike to school, say "hi" to friends, act human, struggle to stay awake, make it through the day without angering anyone, say "bye" to friends, go home, zone out, and then sleep. Wake up the next morning, wash, rinse, and repeat.

Every. Single. Day.

Sometimes, I even had *dreams* of sitting in class working on an assignment. Ugh, that's the *worst*. Even my *dreams* were boring!

I got my tablet off the ground and wiped the grass off it. The screen flickered to life, showing me the time. Surprisingly, I still had about ten minutes until school started. Stashing my Holo Pen behind my ear, I scanned the grass for the brown paper sack that had my lunch.

"Here ya go," some kid said from behind me.

I didn't recognize the voice, but that was normal when you went to school with a thousand other sixth graders.

The sack was torn open. The kid held the ripped bag, a sandwich and carrots, and a note my mom had written that probably said how proud of me she was and that her love for me was forever.

"Thanks," I said, taking everything out of the kid's hands.

"Weird note," he said, glancing down at the paper on top of the food. "It's, like, gibberish or something. Is that another language?"

"Um," I said, looking over the lawn for my book bag. "It's, like, a secret code and stuff. Top-secret information for my eyes only. Government stuff."

"Oh really?" he said with a cocked eyebrow. "A top secret note stuffed into your school lunch?"

"Yep."

"Right," he said as he walked away.

The front doors of the school must had finally opened because everyone was pushing themselves into the lobby.

"Like zombies after brains," I said.

The kid who handed me my lunch was right though. The note from my mom was written in code. It was actually something our family had done for several generations. It was our own way of communicating with each other. It was lame, and it was simple, but if you didn't know what it was, it would look like a bunch of hieroglyphics from a pyramid wall.

I found my book bag in the grass back where I had jumped off my bike, all rumpled up and sad looking.

Scooping it up by one of the straps, I dropped my tablet into it. The rest of my lunch I put into the front pocket of the bag. Other than those few things, my book bag was completely empty, which was the way I liked it – lightweight and easy to carry.

Someone else walked up behind me. I knew because I could hear their footsteps in the grass.

"Nice crash, dummy," the kid said.

I spun around, hoisting my book bag over my right shoulder.

There, standing in front of me, was a robot about my height. On top of the robotic body sat a small glass case with a squid inside, staring right at me.

It was my best friend, Beck.

And he was a squid.

03

The Way It Is

My name is Max.

I'm a sixth grader at Buchanan School.

The year… 2099.

Yep, it's the future.

But the future is the only the future to anyone *not* living in the future.

What's that mean? It means we get all the cool stuff before anyone else.

Dr. Tenderfoot also had a vision that squids would walk among humans someday. Everyone knew that the squid species was intelligent, but it wasn't until Tenderfoot found ways to communicate with them that we knew it for sure.

Back in the fifties, the *twenty-fifties*, Dr. Tenderfoot created his own species of squids named Tenderfoot Squids, or *Tendersquids*.

It was known as the Great Squid Awakening.

Dr. Tenderfoot created the robotic costume that squids used to walk and talk among humans. He called it the Tenderfoot Shell. That's the thing Beck was using when he walked up to me.

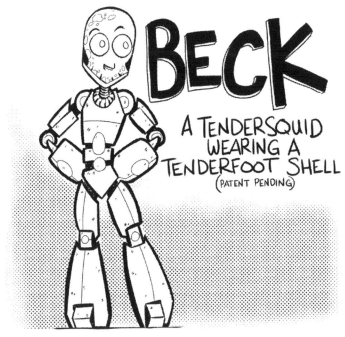

BECK

A TENDERSQUID
WEARING A
TENDERFOOT SHELL
(PATENT PENDING)

Tenderfoot singlehandedly brought the human race – and the squid species – into the future with his creativity and his vision. But sadly, he disappeared soon after the Great Squid Awakening, back in 2062.

Nobody knew where he went. Some believed he froze himself so he could be unfrozen thousands of years in the future. Some believed he traveled into deep space to explore strange new worlds, to seek out new life and new civilizations, to boldly go... well, you know the rest. Some people even believed he invented time travel and had gone into the future.

But whatever happened, to the sixth graders at Buchanan School, he was just an old dude who disappeared way before they were born.

So what's the future look like?

Hover cars? Yes. *Flying* cars? No. Hovering off the ground is cool. Flying through the air is still left to airplanes.

Hover bikes or hover boards? Yes, those exist, but almost nobody has them. Turns out it's cheaper and easier to use bikes and skateboards that have real *wheels*.

Teleporters? Yes, but they're so huge and expensive that only the government uses them, and even then, I'm not sure how much. There are only, like, five of them in the world, and I hear it's a dangerous game every time one was used.

Cities on the moon? Yes, but no big ones.

Cities on Mars? Not cities. More like small towns. One of the first people on Mars was a children's writer or something. I think he won some prize to travel there.

Time travel? Nope. Think about it. If time travel was ever invented, we'd already have seen some visitors from the future, right? I mean, I guess they could keep it a secret, but what fun is that? If I traveled back in time, I'd make such a ruckus about how I was from the future!

I'd be like, "*Look at me! I am from the future! I am the best that humanity has to offer!*"

Holograms? Yes. They're practically built into our everyday lives.

The Holo Pen is an example of that. It's more of a stylus, which is a fancy way of saying "stick." It's our "everything" device.

We use it to write notes on our school tablets. We can also use them for holographic video chatting since it had a tiny projector at the top, which doubles as a flashlight. A small camera is built into the side to record video... which was why everyone was pointing their pens at me when I fell off my bike earlier.

If we don't feel like using the holographic display, we can tuck the pen behind our ear and use it as a simple phone. One end has the speaker, and the other end has the microphone.

And the pens are also used to keep track of where students are in the school. There's a little GPS tracking chip built into each one.

THE
HOLO PEN

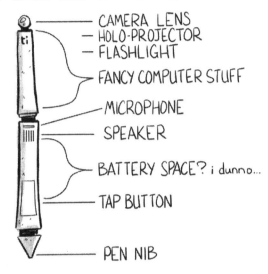

CAMERA LENS
— HOLO-PROJECTOR
— FLASHLIGHT

FANCY COMPUTER STUFF

MICROPHONE

SPEAKER

BATTERY SPACE? i dunno...

TAP BUTTON

PEN NIB

What happens if we lose the Holo Pen? The school simply gives us a new one. They're super cheap.

Other than the Holo Pen, there's no need for paper and pencils anymore, but some kids still have them to write notes to each other. Instead of paper textbooks, we just have a single tablet with our Holo Pen. Every book, every assignment, every report, is all done on the tablet. Mostly.

See? Not *too* futuristic.

That is, if you ignore the talking squid standing in front of me holding my bike.

04

Still outside before school.

I took my bike from Beck, who was trying to hide his laughter. If he could blink, I bet he'd be squeezing his eyes shut.

"Thaaanks!" I said, faking a smile. "I'd like to thank the academy for believing in me, and I'd also like to thank you for being so reckless with my life."

"Dude," Beck said, lifting his robot hands up. "I swear I just forgot about the '*BAIL*' button."

"Squids have awesome memories!" I said. "And you're like, a genius squid among all the other Tendersquids!"

Beck leaned back, pretending to huff on his robotic fingertips and brushing them off on his chest like it was no big deal. "Even the best of us have our moments."

I wasn't stretching the truth about Beck being a genius. He really was smart for a sixth grader.

He once hacked the video screens in the school and made them play cartoons all day long for a week. They tried to fix it right away, but whatever Beck did wasn't easy to fix.

And Beck did all that from *inside* his Tenderfoot Shell. He somehow got control of the school's video system without ever getting out of his seat.

If there was anyone in the school who wanted a life of adventure *more* than me, it'd be Beck. It was probably why we were best friends. We both wanted a little more excitement out of the lives we'd been given.

"Anyways," Beck said, wiping caked dirt off the seat of my bike. "I'm sorry I forgot about that button. The only reason why I'm laughing is 'cause you're okay."

I sniffed hard, like a warrior after battle. "It's cool," I said. "At least my bike's alright."

"Well, there's that little bit right there," Beck said, tapping a spot on the handlebars. "The water fountain took more damage than your bike though. I'm afraid that thing has fountained its last water."

The fountain Beck was talking about was completely wrecked.

"Perfect," I said sarcastically.

"But your bike didn't take much of a beating!" Beck said joyfully, still tapping the same spot on the handlebars. "All it got was this little dent on the metal."

Looking at the spot where Beck was tapping, I saw the logo from the water fountain embedded right onto the metal. It was an infinity symbol – the one that looked like a sideways eight.

"Oh well," I said. "At least the rest of the bike is alright. Looks like your thrusters weren't hurt either."

Beck knelt down to inspect the thrusters. "Mmm," he said. "Nice. There's even enough air in them to try the jump one more time. What d'ya say?"

"No way," I said, aware that my whole body ached with pain. "Flirting with death once a day is enough for me. Plus when the principal gets wind of this, I'll probably get locked up in The Freezer for the rest of the day."

Kids called detention 'The Freezer' because the temperature was always set to "ice cubes" in that room.

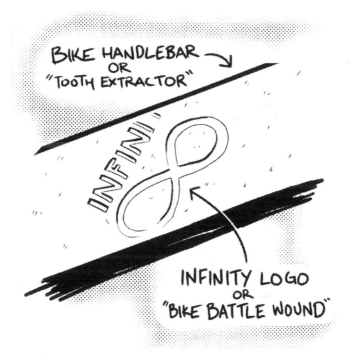

BIKE HANDLEBAR
OR
"TOOTH EXTRACTOR"

"INFINI'

INFINITY LOGO
OR
"BIKE BATTLE WOUND"

"The fail was pretty epic," Beck said. "You might've baby'd out at the end, but at least you gave those kids a show. Pretty sure I saw another Tendersquid ink himself."

"Oh, gross," I laughed. "What happens if you do that?"

Beck sighed, knocking gently on his glass helmet. "Nothing much," he said. "It just takes forever to switch the salt water out, especially when you can't see where you're walking."

"Bummer," a girl's voice said.

I recognized the voice and felt embarrassed. It was Lexi, who had watched my totes epic crash into the wall.

"Yo," I said, trying to avoid eye contact with Lexi, but failing miserably. My eyes kept going back and forth between the ground and her face.

"Hi, Max," she said, smiling. Then she touched my elbow. "Are you okay?"

And just like that, I felt better.

Lexi was another sixth grader at Buchanan School. We've had every class together since the third grade, and I *might* or *might not* have a huge crush on her.

It was one of those things I didn't need to admit because it was totes obvi to anyone with half a brain. She knew it. I knew it. The whole school knew it. As long as nobody talked about it, it was cool.

Standing next to Lexi was a half Japanese girl named Bloom Otsuka.

BLOOM OTSUKA

Bloom and I go way, *way* back – best friends since babies. Our parents knew each other, so Bloom and I spent a lot of time growing up together. She was like my sister.

Bloom was also the toughest girl I knew, which made sense because she had five older brothers who treated her like their youngest brother. That meant there was a lot of wrestling and roughhousing in their home.

Not only that, but she also had a bionic arm. She lost her real arm in a car accident when she was, like, two or three years old and had it replaced with a Tenderfoot model. The bionic arm worked perfectly, like it was real. If she was wearing a long-sleeved shirt and gloves, you wouldn't even know she had it. Unless you wanted to arm-wrestle her.

Do not arm wrestle Bloom. You *will* lose.

"What's that junk on your face?" Bloom said, looking at me funny.

"Apple, I think?" I said. "Rotten apple."

"Who's throwing rotten apples at you?" Bloom said, defensively. She looked around and shouted at the few kids who were still by the front doors of the school. "*Who did this?*"

"Relax," I said. "I'm pretty sure nobody threw it."

"Then how'd it get on your face?"

"I'unno. I think a bird dropped it on me."

"Sick," she said, and shook her head. "So what trick are ya gonna do today?"

"Already did it. Already failed," I said.

"You didn't wimp out, did you?" Bloom said, placing her hands on her hips.

"I didn't *wimp* out, okay?" I said. "I only jumped ship because I found out at the last second that the safety features weren't up to code, alright?"

"*Riiiiiight*," Bloom sang. "The only stunt you ever went through with was the first one, and I'm pretty sure the whole school remembers how that ended."

Bloom was talking about the same accident Lexi had yelled about earlier. I won't say exactly what I was trying to do because it's embarrassing, but it involved my skateboard and a trampoline.

But ever since that first stunt... I always flinched at the last second because I was afraid of getting hurt.

"I've done *more* than *one* stunt," I said, waving my hands around.

"You've *shown up* at more than one stunt, yes," Bloom said. "But you always bail at the end, and then a bunch of stuff

21

gets wrecked, and you've got nothing to show for it. Beck always ends up taking your place, which is awesome 'cause he nails them every time."

"Boom," Beck said, bumping fists with Bloom. The two metallic fists bumping made a small "*CLINK*" sound.

I shook my head, frustrated because Bloom might've been right. I was the kid who always made plans for stunts but never went through with them.

Some daredevil, huh?

Lexi's eyes softened like she felt sorry for me. "Guys, c'mon. These kinds of things aren't easy, and besides, I think it's best for Max to chicken out at the end because it's the safe thing to do."

I knew Lexi was just trying to be helpful, but her words hurt like staples under my fingernails.

The students of Buchanan always gathered around when I announced a stunt, but it wasn't because they wanted to be shocked and awed by my success. It was because they wanted to laugh and point at my crashes.

It was becoming a joke that I couldn't follow through with things, but that morning, jumping over the bike rack… that was *supposed* to be different.

At least, I *wanted* it to be different.

To be honest, when I woke that morning, I was excited because I felt like *something amazing* was going to happen, like I was electrified because of what fate had in store for me.

I guess that electric feeling was for nothing. Fate was a cruel bully laughing at me from behind the looking glass, telling her friends to come and see the loser.

Why are you so mean, fate? *Why?*

05

The hallways. 8:10 AM.

Inside the school, I managed to avoid the staring eyes by keeping my own eyes glued to the tops of my shoes. Not, like, for real though… what I meant was that I was *looking* at my shoes.

Too bad I couldn't keep my *ears* glued to my shoes. No, wait, that saying doesn't work for ears.

As I walked down the hallway, I could hear kids joke about how I bombed the stunt before school. Some of them were unkind, but some, the crueler ones, were just plain mean.

A couple kids even slapped my back, thanking me for giving them something to talk about.

A few were nice about it, encouraging and stuff, but at that point, it was hard to tell the difference between the honest kids and the sarcastic ones.

I finally made it to my locker. There wasn't anything I needed to store in it since everything I needed for class was in my book bag, but I had to change my blazer since the one I was wearing was covered in grass stains and smelled like dirt.

It was only in the last few years that Buchanan School made kids wear uniforms. Somewhere along the line, someone thought if we all had the same clothes, then there wouldn't be a problem with wearing the *wrong* things.

Don't ask me what the *wrong* things were… post-apocalyptic armor?

Someone bumped into me from behind. It was a kid named Chuck. I knew who he was because he came to school everyday wearing a hat made out of tinfoil, shouting about some crazy new theory that meant the end of the world. He called himself Nunchuck Chuck and claimed to be a master at the nunchucks.

23

Nunchuck Chuck's voice sailed over everyone's head. "The shampoo is a sham! It's *poo*, people! It says it right in the name!"

BOYS' UNIFORM   GIRLS' UNIFORM   POST APOCALYPTIC ARMOR

He was definitely one of the weirder kids at Buchanan. Stumbling, he disappeared around the corner.

The walls in the hallway flashed bright, which meant that a video would be played over the walls shortly. My heart beat faster.

At Buchanan School, every hallway wall had a video projection unit installed near the ceiling, which turned the entire wall into a screen. Seemed pointless until you saw it in action.

Because the walls were interactive, you could receive messages right on the surface of your locker if you had your Holo Pen with you.

The walls displayed the correct direction to walk if you were lost. Halls that were off-limits would light up with red, while the halls that were open would light up green.

The school could also request a student to come to the principal's office by displaying their picture in every hallway until the student saw the message. It kind of felt like a "Most Wanted" digital poster whenever that happened.

And because of the damaged water fountain out front, I was counting down the seconds until my face popped up on every wall of the school.

So when the message started playing, I let out a sigh of relief.

On the walls was a video of Principal Green. She wasn't your typical principal. She was young and much prettier than other principals I'd seen before.

"Good morning, everyone!" Principal Green said with a smile. "I just wanted to remind all staff that the science club opened a time capsule this morning. Don't forget to tune in when homeroom starts so they can show us what they've taken out of it. Should be exciting because this is the *oldest* capsule we've unearthed yet! As always, students can participate and ask questions using their Holo Pens after the presentation."

The camera cut to footage of the science club carefully retrieving a time capsule from the hole they dug outside the school.

The principal continued. "I've taken a peek at some of their stuff, and I think you'll all enjoy seeing how kids lived nearly a hundred years ago. You'll be shocked at just how much paper was used when printing textbooks and notebooks. Seriously, wow."

The hallway walls blinked again, and Principal Green's face was gone.

I realized I was still standing in front of my open locker. I stared at the clean blazer inside, and then my eyes went to the tall stack of unused stickers at the bottom of the locker.

I had about a hundred stickers, all from rock bands and comic books. I bought them because they were cheap and an easy way to show off the things I love, except... I never stuck them anywhere. It was too much pressure because I needed them to be in the perfect spot. So, I had built an impressive collection of unstuck stickers.

Bloom always made fun of me for them. It wasn't like I was embarrassed about the stickers, but she was the only one who knew about them.

After switching blazers, I slammed my locker shut, and made my way to homeroom, weaving between the last few students still in the hallway.

I couldn't help but feel like the walls would still shoot up an image of my handsome mug at any second. Like walking faster was gonna stop that from happening, right?

"Max!" Beck's voice called out.

Beck jogged to catch up. We had the same homeroom together, so we were headed in the same direction.

"Those SPUDs find you?" Beck asked.

"What?" I said. "They sent SPUDs after me? I thought they'd just use the walls to call me to the principal's office."

"I don't know," Beck said. "A couple SPUDs stopped me at my locker and asked if I knew where you were – said they'd already checked your locker, and you weren't there."

"I must'a just missed them," I said.

THIS THING IS A **SPUD.**

IT STANDS FOR STUDENT PATROL UNIT.

THE "D" DOESN'T STAND FOR ANYTHING.

"SPUD" JUST SOUNDS BETTER THAN "SPU."

A SPUD was the latest and greatest thing from Tenderfoot Industries. SPUD stood for "Student Patrol Unit." The "D" didn't stand for anything, but saying "SPUD" sounded better than saying "SPU."

They were small robots that stood about two feet tall and were being tested at Buchanan as a way to help students and staff. Basically, they were really short, clumsy, and expensive hall monitors.

They were sent out to find troublesome kids when they needed to go to the principal's office.

And apparently they were trying to find *me*.

06

Homeroom. 8:15 AM.

Beck and I made it to class just as the bell rang.

"On time!" Beck said loudly, dropping into his desk.

The homeroom teacher, Mr. Carter, folded his arms and gave Beck the evil eye.

I took the empty seat in front of my best friend, finally able to relax because I made it to class without seeing a SPUD *and* without seeing my face on a wall.

Score.

Mr. Carter stood at his desk and fiddled with the keyboard, squinting at the computer screen in front of him. His fingers were typing slowly, like his brain was taking forever to send the signal for them to move. He was clearly getting frustrated.

"Rotten stinkin' computers that don't work the way they're supposed to," he said under his breath, but loudly enough for the whole class to hear. "Just work, ya dumb machine!"

Everyone fell completely silent, listening to Mr. Carter whisper sweet insults at his computer as he tried bringing up the video feed Principal Green had encouraged us to watch.

"I swear," he said like his computer was alive. "If you don't start working soon, I'll unplug you without a second thought. You *want* that? You wanna get unplugged? Just *work* already!"

Some giggles sprouted up across the room, me included.

But mine was a *manly* giggle.

Mr. Carter tightened his lips. "Why couldn't we just keep our old holographic displays? Those things worked flawlessly, but nooooooo... Tenderfoot Industries wants to poison the school with new junk that's barely been tested and—" he stopped, pounding his fist onto the keyboard.

The video wall flickered to life.

Mr. Carter raised his arms and shook his head. He had that "*Of course!*" look on his face as he sank into his seat.

The whole wall at the front of the classroom displayed what was happening with the science club. There were ten kids seated at a round table with a chunky time capsule resting in the middle.

The capsule was already opened and the top was resting right next to it. On the table in front of the capsule was everything that had been stuffed into the world's slowest time machine – the kind of time machine that travels at the boring speed of normal time.

I kinda zoned out. Most of what the science club kids were talking about was lame.

"*Blah blah blah history, blah blah blah old school junk, blah blah blah such simple lives, blah blah blaaaaaah.*"

Math textbooks filled with doodles. Small metal rectangles that played music or made phone calls or something. Articles of clothing that only looked a little

brighter than what kids wore in 2099. A newspaper.
Someone's stamp collection. Someone else's favorite book. A
second stamp collection. A bottle of soda. A Twinkie that still
looked fresh. A purse filled with coins and paper money.

Pieces of jewelry, a couple watches, some shiny discs
that had movies on them. And the last thing on the table was a
paper envelope that probably used to be white.

Typical stuff, y'know?

I guess it *was* kind of funny to think that people used to
watch movies that were on discs.

Finally, the science club thanked everyone for watching,
and the video cut out. It took Mr. Carter another minute to
figure out how to switch the video wall off.

The second he did, the lights flipped back on, and a
robotic voice came from the door.

I looked over my shoulder just in time to see two SPUDs
standing in the doorway. Without wasting a second, I slid off
my chair and scooted across the carpet so Beck was blocking
their view.

"Hide me!" I pleaded to my best friend. "They gotta be here because of the water fountain!"

One of the SPUDs mumbled something, but all I recognized was my name.

"What?" Mr. Carter said loudly. "Max? Yeah, he's right— oh, wait. I *thought* he was there…"

Beck spoke up right away. "Yeah, he was here a few minutes ago, but ducked out because he had to, uh…" Beck paused, looking at me for an answer.

I shook my head back and forth quickly because I didn't know what to tell him.

With a smile, Beck looked back at Mr. Carter slowly. "Poop," he said, trying to hide a laugh. "He said he had to… drop a *biscuit* in the *basket*, and he couldn't wait for a hall pass."

Everyone in class laughed.

"*Really?*" I whispered to my best friend. "*Betrayer!*"

"You didn't tell me what to say!" Beck whispered back.

But what Beck said had worked. The two SPUDs at the door apologized for bothering the class and stepped back into the hallway.

I was safe, at least for the moment.

Sneaking back into my chair like some kind of criminal, I pushed against the seat until I was fully sitting up. I could feel the students staring at me again, so I just looked down, slightly embarrassed.

"Um, dude?" Beck said, tapping my shoulder.

"Yeah?" I said, still looking at my desk like it was the most interesting thing in the world.

"Busted," Beck said, pointing past my shoulder at the front wall.

"What?" I said, confused.

Keeping my head down, I raised my eyebrows and followed Beck's finger. My handsome school picture was up on the screen about four-feet wide and six-feet tall. A fake smile. Both eyes half shut.

Worst. Picture. Ever.

Again, for like the tenth time that morning, I was what everyone was laughing at.

The wall also showed my name and directions for me to report to the principal's office immediately.

07

The hallways. 8:30 AM.

I hoisted my book bag over my shoulder and trudged to the door, taking as much time as I could because getting called to the principal's office was never a good thing.

It's never, like, because you won a thousand bucks or something cool like that.

Nope. Nine out of ten times, I got called down because I did something dumb. The tenth time was because I forgot my Holo Pen at home, and the school wanted to make sure I wasn't ditching.

The two SPUDs that had come asking for me were now patiently waiting as I finally walked through the door. Both of them had glowing blue eyes on their faces, which weren't really faces, but more like television screens that *displayed* their faces.

"Nice knowin' ya!" Beck shouted.

Just before the homeroom door closed, I heard the rest of the kids laugh.

"What's this about?" I asked one of the SPUDs.

The SPUD started walking down the hall, speaking with a robotic voice. "*Principal Green would like to see you.*"

"I get that," I said. "But why?"

"*So that Principal Green can see you,*" the SPUD answered, totally *not* answering my question.

SPUDs weren't the smartest machines in the world.

I patted the air with my open hands like I was pumping some brakes. "Whoa, whoa, whoa," I said. "Don't I have the right to what this is all about?"

One of the SPUDs spun around quickly, accidentally bumping the second SPUD, knocking it to the ground.

As soon as the SPUD fell, his arms and legs detached from his body, like a flimsy toy that broke apart when it hit the floor.

It wasn't weird because SPUDs were designed to do exactly that. Those things were as weak as sandcastles.

When Tenderfoot Industries first introduced the idea of putting SPUDs into schools, parents made some noise about how those tiny little robots could accidentally hurt children since, y'know, SPUDs *were* machines.

Tenderfoot Industries' solution was to make SPUDs easily fall apart. The main parts of their body were held together by magnets, so the SPUDs never actually broke. They just lost their limbs.

Every once in a while, you'll see some kid soccer punt a SPUD. Part of me felt sad when that happened, like the SPUD was getting bullied or something, but then I remembered... it was just a machine.

THIS GUY FELL APART, BUT DON'T WORRY. HE DOESN'T CARE... ...HE'S JUST A ROBOT.

There was one other requirement stipulated by parents before allowing the little robot helpers in the school – the SPUDs had to be programed with two rules...

"Do not touch the students," and *"Obey any 'stop' command a student or teacher gives."*

The *"stop"* command was used if a student *ever* felt scared of a SPUD. The instant the student said it, the SPUD would stop in place. It wasn't the best system, but it worked.

The SPUD on the floor was wobbling back and forth, trying to find its arms and legs.

"Should we help him?" I asked the other SPUD like it was human.

"Negative," the SPUD said. *"Help is on the way."*

As soon as the robot said it, I heard the sound of other SPUDs walking down the hallway. I stepped around them and made my way to the principal's office.

Glancing over my shoulder, I saw the SPUDs taking care of their fallen robot friend. It was such a weird thing to watch - robots helping other robots get back on their feet. I wondered if they felt sad for the SPUD who needed help, and I wondered if the SPUD who needed help felt embarrassed like I had earlier that morning.

"This way," my SPUD said. *"We mustn't keep Principal Green waiting."*

The walls to the hallway blinked, creating a path of green arrows for me to follow. The spot on the wall next to me had my picture on it again, letting me know the green arrows were for me.

I knew this was in case I needed help figuring out where the principal's office was, but it just felt like the school building was pointing fingers at me.

"Really?" I said. "Was that necessary?"

"You appeared confused," the SPUD explained. *"I am only here to help you."*

I nodded. "Right. Thanks for *that*."

The SPUD escorted me the rest of the way back to the front lobby. Not like I couldn't have made it there myself, but that's what SPUDs were built for.

In the lobby, the little robot turned and nodded its head to me before taking a place against the wall, under the tinted glass windows of the cafeteria.

Since I had been called to the office using the video walls, it meant that every wall in the school was showing my face with the same message. Everyone knew I was there.

A bunch of kids even pressed their faces against the cafeteria windows, ready to see me get scolded for the destruction of school property.

"This way, Max," a man said from the office door. I didn't know his name, but I had seen him a million times working in the office. He was part of the staff.

I paused. I hated walking into a situation without knowing what was about to go down. "Can you tell me what this is about?" I asked.

"Not my business to know," he said. "Principal Green just needs to speak with you about something. I wouldn't worry about it. There aren't any police here, so you're good, but the grim reaper might be around... pretty sure you couldn't see him if he was though." He laughed at his own joke.

"Nice," I said under my breath.

"I'm only messing with you," the man said, holding the door open for me. "But there's no sense worrying about it until you speak with her first."

I walked through the door to the front office and headed straight for the back, to Principal Green's office. Across the hall from her was the nurse's station – a place I was way too familiar with.

A bench was set up just outside the principal's office. I dropped my book bag on top of it and took a spot at the far end, just far enough that Principal Green wouldn't notice me right away.

The bench was old and made of wood. I wasn't sure, but the thing had to be a hundred years old. The metal bolts were crusty and brown, and the whole thing felt sticky, like it was plastered with a gross polish.

The door to my left swung open, and Principal Green stuck her head out. "Where in the heck is that kid?" she mumbled before she saw me. "Oh, Max, there you are."

I tightened a smile.

The principal held out her open hand, aiming it back into her office. "Why don't you have a seat in here. We need to have a little talk."

I know, right? What an amazing day it was shaping up to be.

08

The principal's office. 8:40 AM.

I shuffled into the principal's office until I was standing at her desk against the far wall. Principal Green had propped her door open and was briskly walking back to the other side of the desk.

The bell to first period had just gone off. Man, that was one of the first times in my life I actually wished I was *in* class.

I was dead meat, and I knew it. Half the school filmed me crashing my bike into the water fountain, and now Principal Green was about to call my parents to let them know they should go coffin shopping for me.

My gut was so uneasy I felt like I was gonna puke.

The principal took a seat in her old leather chair, rubbing against the surface and making it sound like a fart. If it were me, I'd spend the rest of the morning trying to recreate the same sound so you'd know it wasn't really a fart, but Principal Green didn't seem to care as she shuffled through some papers on her desk, mumbling softly to herself.

Ugh! I couldn't take it anymore! I could feel beads of sweat collect on my forehead as I waited for her to dish out my hard-boiled punishment! So my brain, being the mega-hyper brain it was, decided to speak before she did.

"I'm so sorry about this morning," I said, feeling disconnected from my body. It was like watching my own confession on television. "It was totally my fault! I shouldn't have bailed, wait no – I shouldn't even have *tried* the stupid stunt to begin with! I take full responsibility, and I—"

The principal leaned forward in her chair. "Wait, what?" she asked.

"The water fountain!" I said. "In front of the school! I'm the one who *accidentally* smashed it up with my bike!" I lifted my finger as if I had a point to make. "The keyword is *accidentally*, and that water fountain probably shouldn't even have been installed at that part of the school."

Principal Green eyeballed me, trying to make sense of what I was saying. I could see it in her eyes – she felt sympathy for me!

"I just couldn't hold it in any longer," I said. "And I'm so thankful you called me in here today. Wow, that was such a weight off my shoulders! I feel like a new kid!" I grabbed my book bag strap around my shoulder and smiled so huge it hurt. "Thanks again for this meeting, Principal Green. A lesson learned is a lesson, um… learned, right? Alrighty then. Good talk! See ya!"

I made it about two steps before the principal spoke.

"Max," she said, slightly concerned. "Have a *seat*, young man."

Defeated, I dropped into the chair in front of her desk. "Yes, ma'am."

The principal picked up a small yellow-stained envelope and waved it at me. "You're here because of this," she said.

I didn't know what to say. "But… I mean… the fountain…"

Principal Green's eyebrows raised as she pressed her lips together. "Uh, yeah, about that. I heard all about the water fountain out front, but didn't know who did it. Destruction of property, Max? That's detention *and* a meeting with your parents."

I hung my head low, gently punching it with the back of my knuckles. "Stupid big mouth. Stupid, stupid big mouth and tiny brain."

Just then, something splattered on the window behind Principal Green. Yellow mush slid down the glass. Across the entire window were the dried splatters of the same thing.

"Did something just poop on your window?" I asked.

Principal Green sighed as she looked out her window. "No, it's not poop. It's mushed up apples. Some bird keeps flying overhead or something and dropping them on the school. I really oughta get someone to clean it up. Smells great, but looks disgusting."

I almost told her about the bird nailing me in the head with the rotten apple, but decided not to. It was too embarrassing, but... what if the birds were launching an attack on the human race? Wasn't it my responsibility to warn everybody? What if they were finally fed up with the fact that we ate chickens and ducks and... uh... nevermind.

The principal turned back toward me, waving the envelope again, but this time, she tossed it so it landed right in my open lap. "Anyways, we'll get to the bit about the broken water fountain and your vacation in detention soon enough, but let's talk about this first."

The envelope in my lap was yellowed and ancient with a musty old book smell to it.

It *looked* familiar.

"What is this?" I asked, holding the envelope in my hand.

"You tell me," the principal said.

I was confused. "Is this some sort of test? Am in trouble for this?"

"No," she laughed. "You're not in any trouble for *this*, at least. That envelope was found in the time capsule this morning."

Right as she said it, I remembered seeing the envelope in the video during homeroom. It was the last thing on the science club kid's table.

I held the envelope over my head so that the light was behind it. I thought maybe I could see what was inside, but the paper was too thick.

"We already opened it," Principal Green said, letting out a small laugh.

"Oh," I said, peeking between the envelope flaps. Another folded sheet of paper was nestled inside. I couldn't read any of the writing, but I saw a couple of pen marks and a scribbled doodle of what looked like a ninja mask.

I gotta be honest – it looked super cool, like the kind of thing a comic book collector would frame.

"There's not much to the letter inside," the principal said. "It's just one sheet with a bunch of sketches of what looks like the school back when the sender was a student," the principal said. "Pretty neat looking stuff, huh?"

I didn't answer. I had already unfolded the sheet of paper from the envelope. There were cool pencil sketches of different parts of the school that I recognized.

"That drawing looks like the cafeteria, doesn't it?" Principal Green said, pointing her finger at the paper. "And look there. It's the cafeteria stage along with hand drawn blueprints of the backstage."

"Funny," I said. "When was this time capsule buried?"

"About eighty-five years ago?" Principal Green said, raising her tone at the end of the sentence, making it sound like she was asking a question. "This building has seen a lot of changes since then, but some of the things in those sketches are still the same."

"Okay," I said, folding the letter shut. The smell of musty paper wafted under my nose. It reminded me of my dad's old comics. "So what's this got to do with me?"

Principal Green smiled, folded her hands, and leaned forward on her desk. "That envelope you're holding? It was buried eighty-five years ago with some pretty specific instructions as to who it was supposed to be delivered to."

The hairs on my arm raised as I ran my fingers across the top of the envelope.

"That envelope..." The principal paused, letting the moment sink in, "was addressed to *you*, Max."

Pop.

Mind. Blown.

09

The principal's office. 8:50 AM.

"You can close your mouth now," Principal Green said. "You're foggin' up the windows."

I was so in shock that I didn't even realize my jaw had dropped. It must've been open for a few seconds, too, because my tongue was dry.

"This was addressed to me?" I said. "How's that even possible? This thing was buried over *eighty* years ago… Is this some kind of joke?"

"It's no joke," the principal said, and then she explained. "It wasn't actually addressed to you *personally*, but it *was* addressed to any living relative of the kid who sent the note, so basically anyone in your family."

"This thing belonged to someone I'm related to?" I said, looking for a name on the outside of the envelope.

"It's not on the envelope. It was on the master list included in the time capsule."

"That's wild…"

Principal Green shuffled through papers on her desk, pushing them toward me. "I had some of the staff research the kid who put that in the capsule to figure out who might be related to him. We didn't expect to find *anyone* related to them to be a *current* student, let alone in the same *grade* as he was."

"So it's a boy," I said.

The papers on Principal Green's desk were scattered about. Pictures of past students lined the pages with their full names under them. Circles were drawn between faces that showed how they were related.

She even had a couple of super old yearbooks opened to the pages with pictures of my relatives circled right on the paper. I recognized the pictures of my parents back when they were students.

It was like a trail leading all the way back to the kid who sent the note I was holding in my hands.

"So what?" I asked. "This was, like, my second great uncle twice removed, related only by marriage, but not really because they were divorced or something weird like that?"

"Nope. *Much* closer than that," Principal Green said with a smile. "Actually, we were thrilled to find that it was your great-*great*-grandfather, Chase Cooper."

I stared at the principal.

The principal stared back at me. I think she was expecting me to say something.

"...who?" was all I could muster up.

"Your name is Max Cooper, is it not?" she asked, obviously rhetorically.

I nodded like a dog, half-asleep. "Uh-huh."

"Well," the principal said, clearly thinking of how to explain the whole thing. "When two people get married, they share the same last name, and their children also have the same last name. Traditionally, the son grows up, gets married, and has kids of his own, who also share the last name, until finally—"

"I know how family trees work," I said, interrupting Principal Green's blunder in thinking I was a five-year-old. "I just... I'm not sure how to feel about this."

"Why?"

"It's a note from my great-great-grandfather, but like, I didn't know him. It's cool that this piece of history is in my family, I guess, but... don't you wanna give this letter to some sciency type of people so they can study it or something? Research and junk?"

Principal Green laughed. "No, this type of thing doesn't interest folks like that. It's not old enough."

And then she slid a single school picture across her desk until it was in front of me.

It was a picture of my great-great-grandfather when he was just a sixth grader at Buchanan School. He would've been my age in the photo.

I stared at the picture of the boy with *super* spiky hair. He *kinda* looked like me, I guess. Not *quite* as dashing, but still a handsome fella.

"But this letter's almost a hundred years old," I said, running my fingers along the edge of the envelope.

CONLEY   CHASE COOPER   RAUB

"Right," she said. "But it's more of a neat collectible. Like a vintage toy or something. We already took a look at it. It's just a bunch of doodles and some gibberish at the top of the page."

I opened the letter again, this time paying attention to the things that were drawn on it. Everything was teeny tiny, like he was only allowed to use one sheet of paper to send to the future.

Chase's sketches were sloppy and scratchy but super cool. There were tiny blueprints of the school, and on the back were diagrams of ninja moves and stuff.

Principal Green was right. The sheet was filled with junky drawings, and the text at the top was crudely scribbled, but oddly familiar. Actually, *too* familiar.

43

The gibberish at the top was the *same* code my family used to write notes to each other. It was the same code my mom used to write that note in my lunch.

"Whoa," I said.

"Maybe you can make sense of it," Principal Green said. "If anything, I'm sure your parents would find it very interesting, but to the science club, that letter is nothing more than a family heirloom. It's worth more to your family than it is to a bunch of sixth grade archeologist wannabes — I mean... not... I didn't mean wannabes. You didn't hear me say that."

I gently set the envelope into my book bag against the back of my tablet, and then looked Principal Green dead in the eye. "I didn't hear you say anything... if I don't have detention for the water fountain incident."

Principal Green didn't break eye contact. She took a deep breath, staring right back at me, almost *through* me.

"That water fountain was gonna get removed anyway," she said, and held out her hand. "Deal."

I grabbed the principal's hand, squeezed it tightly, and shook it like a businessman.

10

The lobby. 9:25 AM.

After leaving Principal Green's office, I sat in the lobby until
first period was over. She said it'd be alright if I skipped the
rest of class. After all, it wasn't everyday someone got a note
from their great-great-grandfather. She thought it was kind of a
big deal, and maybe it was, but I just wasn't feeling it.

 I mean, Chase went to Buchanan almost eighty years
before I did. There was no way we'd have anything in
common. I wondered if we even would've been friends.

 Anyway, sitting in the lobby gave me time to decode the
message at the top of the front page anyway.

Cracking the code wasn't quite as easy as I thought it'd be. It was *almost* like the code my family used, but not quite the same. Makes sense though since the message was, like, eighty-years-old. Languages change over time and so do codes apparently.

It worked just like any other simple message where the letters in the alphabet were mixed up, but our code involved numbers and dots to make it more difficult.

It took until a few minutes before the bell rang for me to finally figure it out. A lot of it was just guessing until I got the letters right.

As the lobby filled with students walking to their lockers, I stared at the front page of the note, reading and re-reading the message I had decoded.

"Hey, Max," Beck said as he walked up.

My brain was so busy thinking that I forgot to respond.

Beck took the spot next to me and looked over my shoulder at the letter. "What's that? Whoa, you're getting love notes on real paper now?"

"No," I answered. "This is from the time capsule they dug up this morning. You'll never believe this, but it was addressed to *me*."

"You're right, I *don't* believe you," Bloom said, stepping out of the sea of students. "Someone sent you a love note from a hundred years ago. Oh, maybe it's your future wife who accidentally traveled back in time and has sent you a message telling you how to rescue her!"

"Is it that?" Beck asked, raising a spot where his eyebrow would be if he had them. "Is that letter from your future wife who sent it from the past?"

Bloom sat on the other side of me, smiling with the corner of her mouth. "And is your future wife's name… Lexi?"

Beck pressed his squid lips together. "Oooooo!" he sang.

"Funny, funny, guys," I said. "And it's not from Lexi *or* my future wife."

"No need to separate the two," Bloom said. "They're the same person."

I rolled my eyes. "Okay, already, we get it. I got a crush on Lexi. I know it. You guys know it. Should we let the whole school know it?"

And like the universe wanted to take another jab at me, Lexi showed up out of nowhere.

"Let the school know what?" Lexi asked, setting her book bag down on the floor.

"What?" I said, frantically. "*Nothing!*"

"No, what were you just talking about?" Lexi said. "You sounded pretty loud about it."

"We were talking about what Bloom thinks is cuter – kittens or newborn babies," I said, lying through my teeth. "She said kittens, and then I asked her why she hated newborn babies so much."

"Whatever!" Bloom smiled. "Tell her what we were *really* talking about, hmmm? I think she'd totally be interested in what your thoughts were on—"

Burying my face in my palms, I cut Bloom's sentence short. "Oh my—*nothing*, okay?" I mumbled, and then quickly changed the subject. I waved the time capsule letter in front of me. "I got this from Principal Green just a little bit ago."

"Oh," Beck said. "Is that why those SPUDs wanted you?"

"I *saw* your face all over the walls," Lexi said. "Did you get in trouble for the water fountain?"

"No," I said. "Um, the principal and I worked out a deal… but the real reason she wanted to see me was because the science club took something out of the time capsule that belonged to my family."

"Spicy," Bloom said. She was on a mission to replace the word "cool" with "spicy." I wasn't sure if it was working. "So that thing is from someone who was related to you?"

I nodded. "My great-great-grandfather, I guess. He used to go to school here, like, *way* back in the day – almost a hundred years ago. He was even in sixth grade when he put this in the capsule."

"Creepy," Lexi said, lifting her forearm up. "Look, I got goose bumps!"

"Goose bumps," Beck repeated. "Such a strange thing human skin does."

"Oh, right," Lexi said. "Sometimes I forget you're a squid."

"Goosebumps ain't anythin' special," Bloom said. "Trust me – y'ain't missin' out on much."

"I never said I felt like I was missing out on anything," Beck said. "I just said it was strange."

"Well, I think the way Tendersquids can change colors is strange," Lexi said.

"It's a defense mechanism," Beck said. "And it's *cool*."

"So that letter's from a hundred years ago?" Bloom said, turning back to me. "Wasn't that when teachers were still allowed to spank students?"

"Uh, no," I said. "I don't think it was *that* long ago."

"So what'd your great-great-grandpa write?" Lexi said. "Is it, like, a page from his history class or something? Y'know, even if he were taking notes from his own current events, they'd still be history to us."

Lexi was clever. Something about the way her brain worked made me feel like my muscles were melting.

"I'm sure it's just a buncha boring mumbo jumbo," Bloom said, putting one foot up on the nook. "You're letting your imagination get the best of you. Come back to reality with the rest of us."

"Why would I choose reality when imagination is so much cooler?" I said. "I don't wanna watch a movie about a dude gettin' a job. I wanna watch a movie where a dude has to fight a dragon!"

Bloom stuck out her tongue. "Mumbo. Jumbo."

"Actually," I said. "I don't think it's just *mumbo jumbo*. I think there's more to it than that."

My friends leaned closer to look. They were more interested than I thought they'd be, and to be honest, I didn't mind the extra attention.

"It's a coded message," I explained. "Along with a bunch of diagrams and blueprints of the school."

"A coded message?" Beck asked, *super* interested all of a sudden. "How do you know what it says?"

"Funny thing," I said. "That's how I know it's really from my own family. The code is one we've used for many generations. It was *a little* different, but, like, 90% of it was the same."

"Whoa," Beck whispered.

"And that's not all," I said, flipping the letter over. "Look at this... it's got all these diagrams of ninja moves."

Everyone leaned even closer, but I folded the letter up before they could get a good look.

It dawned on me that I was holding something powerful, something way cool to my friends. If I showed them some doodles and one coded message, they'd stop caring pretty quickly.

I wanted to stretch it out as long as I could. "So yeah, coded messages," I said. "Like, *a bunch* of coded messages on this thing. Gonna take me at least a couple weeks to get through it all."

Beck's eyes drifted, and I knew I had him hooked. "So awesome," he whispered.

"How much have you decoded?" Lexi asked.

"Not much yet," I said. "I only finished the first line before the bell rang."

"What's it say?" Bloom said, unimpressed. "Is it some kind of lame poem?"

I laughed. "No. I think it's a *riddle*."

"A *riddle?*" Beck repeated.

"A *riddle*," I said a second time. The riddle was so short that I had it memorized. "It said, 'Search the dungeon to find your fate; life begins at 48. Cheers.'"

The number 8 was written at such a weird angle that it looked crooked – like someone had yanked the paper away as it was being written down. It almost looked sideways.

"What's the dungeon?" Bloom said.

My friends looked at each other, confused.

"Does Buchanan School have a basement?" Lexi said.

Bloom shook her head. "No. There's a second floor and a third floor but no basement."

"So then, is he talking about the locker rooms or something?" I said. "Could that be the dungeon?"

"The boy's locker room maybe," Bloom said. "The girl's locker room is a palace."

Beck was staring at nothing as a smile grew on his face.

Bloom narrowed her eyes and nodded her head at Beck. "What's his deal? Why's he smiling like that? Beck, *why* are you smiling like you're farting? Squids don't fart. Wait, do squids fart?"

Beck shook his head, and then looked at the rest of us. "Dudes…" he paused. "There *is* a lower level here."

"Huh," I said. "This letter just got a billion times more interesting."

11

We were still sitting in the nook of the lobby, stunned by what Beck had just said.

Other students were walking back and forth, passing us, talking and laughing with their friends. Buchanan School gave students fifteen minutes between each class so kids wouldn't feel rushed to make it to their lockers and then to class.

"What do you mean there's a lower level?" Bloom asked. "We've been here all year. Have any of you even *heard* about a lower level?"

Lexi and I shook our heads at the same time and at the same speed as if we were connected by a string.

"You've never heard about it because it's been closed off," Beck said. "The only way to get down there is through a maze of walls inside the school. Not even the elevator goes down anymore."

"So how do you know about it?" Bloom asked, suspicious.

"I might've run across the entrance once or twice when I was exploring."

"You explore the dark parts of the school?"

"Of course. Max and I are action junkies, right? We're all about adventures! How can someone call themselves an adventurer if they never explore strange new places?"

"He's got a point," I said.

"So why's it closed off?" Bloom said.

Beck shrugged his robot shoulders. "The story is that some kid pulled a prank so legendary that it completely flooded the lower level. I don't know exactly when, but there was something about it being around Christmas time? Or a holiday? I don't know – *something* about Christmas. The

51

school cleaned it, but it was too messed up to save so they closed it up after that."

"There ya have it," Bloom said, setting her foot down. "Sounds like you've reached a dead end."

"How's that a dead end?" Beck asked.

"I'm sure there's not an empty basement down there anymore," Bloom explained. "The smart thing for them to do would've been to fill it with cement or something."

"Can they do that?" I said.

"I'unno," Bloom said, looking at the clock on the wall. "Oh, dudes, time to rock! The bell's gonna ring in a second."

Lexi jumped to her feet. She took a step, but stopped and glanced over her shoulder at me. "See ya, Max. Don't do anything dumb, alright?"

I gave her a thumbs-up and a smile.

Once Bloom and Lexi left, Beck tapped the letter in my hand. "So... we headin' to the dungeon then?"

For a second, I considered it, but just couldn't bring myself to agree to go down there. "I dunno, dude," I said honestly. "It doesn't sound like the safest thing ever, and Bloom was right about the bell ringing soon. Second period's about to start."

"But what if I said..." Beck paused. "*Please?*"

I laughed. "Really? That's your way of getting me to do something?"

Beck shuffled his robotic feet. "Maybe? I dunno. Every human reacts differently when I say that."

I dropped the letter back into my book bag. "Yeah, no. I think I'm gonna have to pass right now. I really should talk to my parents about this whole thing. I think they'll wanna see the letter from... I guess it would be my dad's great-grandfather."

"But, dude!" Beck said. He spoke with a whisper, but it somehow sounded like he was yelling. "That letter! That letter is the adventure we've been waiting for! You said there were *tons* of other coded messages on it! We could be searching forever!"

"Yep," I said, trying to smile. "Tons of other codes is definitely what I said."

But even still. There might not have been a *ton* of other coded messages, but there was definitely *one* that needed to be investigated.

All our lives we talked about how adventurous and brave we were… about how we were the risk takers and wanted more from life… and finally, there it was, sitting in my lap.

But I was afraid of doing anything about it. Afraid of doing something different when I didn't know what would happen. I *wanted* it, but the fear in my belly was keeping me from moving.

"I can't," I said finally. It felt good to make the decision.

Beck continued. "That thing is a treasure hunt! It's a treasure hunt sent from the past. Our chance to finally *do* something crazy! To do something real!"

I didn't know what to say, so I said nothing.

"Your great-great-grandfather, what's his name?" Beck asked with wide eyes.

"Chase," I said.

"Chase…" Beck repeated. "He's probably rolling around in his grave right now because he's given you a chance to do something *awesome*, and you're just… just… *wasting* it!"

I wasn't sure why Beck was so hardcore about searching the dungeon. He was a passionate kid, er *squid*, but I had never seen him act like that.

"Chase is passing down his legacy," Beck said. "He's trying to give you something of his own…"

"Okay, I get that," I said, "but even Chase wouldn't mind me talking to my parents about it first."

Beck sighed heavily. He sank down in his glass helmet, defeated. "Alright," he nodded slowly. "It's cool. We can wait… I just thought… y'know, that letter was like a spark of color in our grey and boring lives."

"I know, but—"

Beck interrupted me. "I'm a Tendersquid," he said. "Which means my lifespan is longer than normal cephalopods, but not by much."

I sat quietly, listening to my best friend. He almost never talked about his feelings. It was… awkward.

"Normal lifespans for squids are two to three years if they're lucky," Beck said. "Tendersquids live to be twenty, sometimes twenty-five years old. When you're twenty-five, you'll have the whole rest of your life ahead of you… but I'll be an old kraken on his death bed…"

53

I stared at the floor.

"Probably living in some oversized aquarium for the elderly," Beck said. "Eating food that humans sprinkle on top of the water…"

Beck was making his point crystal clear. I felt sorry for the kid, but I knew that was exactly what he wanted.

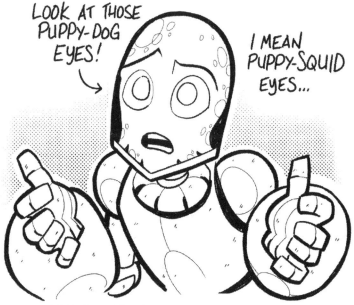

LOOK AT THOSE
PUPPY-DOG
EYES!

I MEAN
PUPPY-SQUID
EYES...

"Alright," I said at last.

"Wondering why my kids never call me," Beck said. "Wondering where the years went… pining for the days of old when I had goals other than simply *waking up* after going to sleep…"

"*Alright*," I said again.

"I wonder if I'll have to use a little propeller to move around," Beck said. "My tentacles prob'ly won't work so good when I get old… oh, man, and the squid diapers? Don't get me started on squid diapers."

"Dude, *alright!*" I said, laughing. "Holy buffalo, just stop with all the old squid talk! I'll go down to the dungeon with you. Just… don't ever say 'squid diapers' ever again, cool?"

"*Spicy*," Beck said joyfully. "So the riddle in your letter said to search the dungeon. Let's start there and figure out step two."

"Sounds like a plan."

"Follow me," Beck said, standing to his robot feet.

I took a deep breath and followed behind my best friend. He seemed to know exactly where he was going so it was easy for me to let him take the lead.

My guts were spinning circles though. I wasn't sure why, but the whole thing made me nervous. Exploring a strange part of the school? Following a clue that my great-great-granddad left me in a letter that was just dug up that morning?

It all sounded crazy, right?

Too bad I had no idea how much crazier things were about to get.

12

The backdoors. 9:45 AM.

The secret hallways in the school weren't as secret as I thought they were going to be. I expected Beck to push a bunch of bricks in a special order that made the wall flip around, but it wasn't like that.

It wasn't like that at all.

The door to the secret hallway was right next to the elevator. I must've passed it hundreds of times walking back and forth through the lobby, but never noticed it before.

Beck had me wait at the door while he went in to make sure we were good. A few minutes had already passed. I was getting worried that someone was going to see me, so I pushed the door open and went in alone. Smart, right?

The hallway on the other side of the door was cold and dark, but dry. The gray walls of exposed cinder blocks loomed over me. You could still see the mortar between each block as they stacked higher and higher.

The hallway wasn't completely abandoned either – that much was clear. Barely visible footprints showed that people still used these hallways to get from one place to another.

Beck was nowhere to be seen.

"Hello?" I whispered, inching my way forward, getting that same freaked out feeling I got when I walked through a haunted house.

I passed several open doors that had SPUD parts hanging from the walls and sprawled out across tables.

Finally, I came to a room full of computer monitors. Beck was standing at the wall of screens.

"Dude!" I said.

Beck spun around, frightened. He shut his eyes and sighed. "You about gave me a heart attack," he said. "I told you to wait at the door!"

"You took forever!" I said, trying to see past my friend. "What're you doing?"

"Nothing!" he said. "I saw this room and wanted to check it out. Sorry I left you alone out there."

"No bigs. Is this where SPUDs get worked on?"

"I think so," Beck said as he walked past me. "This is where they come when they need repairs. I'm pretty sure one of these rooms is also where they get assembled."

"Wow. I never realized until just now that SPUDs appear out of nowhere."

"Yeah. These hallways go all around the school. There're exits in tons of different parts. They use these halls to get around."

"So you've checked this place out before?" I asked.

"Mm-hmm," Beck said. "I saw a SPUD use one of those doors, and I *needed* to know where he was going. This room is where their mainframe is."

"Cool," I said, trying to act like I understood. "Um… what's that?"

"It's like their brain. They're all connected to the mainframe, so I guess it's more like a *shared* brain. They're like ants, and the mainframe is the queen… except that the mainframe doesn't think for itself."

"Huh?" I said, still befuddled.

Cool word that is… *befuddled.* Is *befuddle* the present tense of befuddled? Befuddling?

I was befuddling over why someone would ever choose high pulp orange juice.

It sounded weird, but I think it was right.

Befuddle…

Befuddled…

You will be *befuddled*…

I will befuddle you!

"Dude!" Beck said, snapping me out of my trance. "You okay?"

"Uh, yeah," I said. "I get distracted pretty easily…"

"Okay, but did you hear *anything* I said?" Beck asked.

"Yeah!" I said, shaking my head. "Nope!"

Beck sighed in his glass helmet. "I said their mainframe's unguarded and completely out in the open. That's why we don't have to worry about anyone seeing us back here. The SPUDs are programmed to operate by themselves."

"Unguarded?" I said. "That just *sounds* like an invitation to mess with it."

"Right?" Beck said, turning the corner. "So… there are exits on this floor, the second floor, and the third floor."

"*And* the dungeon," I said.

"*And* the dungeon," Beck repeated. I could tell from his voice that he was smiling when he said it. "But we'll have to find our way down there… I just need to remember where I saw those stairs."

"How hard can it be to find stairs?" I said, running my fingers along the gritty surface of the brick wall. I wondered who else touched the same spot I was touching. The building had been around for so long; if the walls could speak, I was sure they'd have crazy stories to tell.

"Not hard," Beck said. "But it's not like I have a map of the school."

"Oh, but I do!" I said, taking the letter out of my book bag.

I unfolded the sheet, wondering how many more times I could do it without the flimsy paper crumbling apart.

Beck watched, waiting patiently as I studied the tiny blueprints, trying to make sense of what my great-great-granddad drew so many years ago.

Finally, I found the drawing that looked like the cafeteria. All I had to do was keep moving to the right until...

"Bingo," I said, tapping the paper gently. "These secret hallways are on this paper!"

I was pumped as I scanned the skinny line drawing of the spot where we stood. The lines moved up the paper, turned right, and then turned right again to a drawing of a huge circular room with a staircase at the back of it.

Beck and I traveled the same path, turning right two more times until we found what we were looking for.

Beck stopped, pointing at an open doorway at the end of our path.

"Look," he said.

The door looked like it opened to a larger room, bigger than any of the rooms we had passed. Plus it wasn't as dark in there as it was in the hallway. A low yellow light softly filled the room.

"Yup, I remember now," Beck said. "The stairs are through there."

I let my best friend take the lead once again since he was kind of familiar with the place.

Once we were inside the room, a weight lifted from my shoulders. I didn't realize how closed in and suffocated I had felt back in the dark hallway. Now that we were out of there, I could breath again.

At the center of the room was a circular wall made of large stones about two feet high. It was covered up with some really old, crusty wooden boards.

"Is that a well?" I said.

"Looks like," Beck said as he marched to the other side of the room.

"What's the school doing with a well at the center of it?"

"Beats me, but it doesn't look like it's been used in forever."

The explorer in me wanted to know what was down in the well, but the middle-aged man in my brain said it was dangerous.

I always imagined the two fighting on my shoulders like one was an angel and the other the devil. They both looked like me, but dressed differently. The explorer looked like some kind of bearded Viking, and the middle-aged version of me wore a plaid suit and tie. Whenever I—

"Dude!" Beck said.

"Sorry!" I shouted as I jogged to the other side of the room. I got caught daydreaming again.

When I reached Beck, he was standing at the front of the staircase. His hand was out, palm-up, as if he were presenting a prize to me.

The stairs went down about six steps to a landing. They must've turned and gone down another six steps into the dungeon. It was dark too, but not completely.

"After you," Beck said.

"Ladies first," I replied.

"Oh, come on, already!" Beck grunted.

I nodded quickly, taking a deep breath. After I let all the air out through my nose, I did what I felt like I was born to do…

I took my first step toward the real adventure.

13

The dungeon. 10:00 AM.

"Search the dungeon to find your fate," I said. "Life begins at 48."

Beck was behind me, studying the walls of the dungeon. We were both using our Holo Pens as flashlights, pointing them in every dark corner.

"Look at all these old lockers," Beck said.

"Yeah," I said. "They look all hardcore and heavy. Like, the metal is super thick compared to the ones we use upstairs. And look at all the old combination locks."

"I bet this place hasn't changed in the last hundred years," Beck said. "Your gramps prob'ly even had classes down here."

"*Great-great*-gramps," I reminded Beck.

It was weird, but Beck was right. The dungeon hadn't been updated in forever. It was almost like we were walking through an oversized time capsule.

Picture frames still hung above the lockers with portraits of students who got straight-A's. The lockers had paint peeling off their doors, but surprisingly there weren't any paint chips on the floor.

Each room we passed was open and dark inside. All the doors had been removed from the classrooms, probably for safety reasons when they sealed the place up.

One of the rooms even had two sets of doors removed. I moved my Holo Pen around inside the room and saw that it was much larger than the rest of the classrooms down there.

It must've been the old orchestra room. I could tell because the floor angled upward toward the back. Since the dungeon had been sealed off, the new orchestra room was up on the third floor.

I looked back down the hall, at all the missing doors on the rooms.

Every single door was gone… except one.

Beck continued to walk down the corridor, waving his Holo Pen back and forth, playing with the way the light reflected off the linoleum floor and metal lockers.

I walked up to the only room with a door and stared at it. The door was made of metal, which surprised me because all the classroom doors upstairs were wood. The metal was dull with a brushed texture all over the surface. And it was clean.

It definitely *wasn't* a door that had been there for two hundred years.

At the bottom of the door was a thin sliver of light. If I had been walking in complete darkness, I would've seen the light escaping on the floor, but since I was pointing my Holo Pen at everything, I had missed it.

The light on the floor seemed to fade in and out, pulsing.

I ran my fingers along the bottom of the door. The air coming from it was cold as ice.

Pushing my ear against the door as quietly as possible, I closed my eyes, hoping I'd hear something cool. But instead, I only heard the soft thumps of my own heartbeat.

I was about to knock, but my knuckles stopped inches away from the metal. I couldn't be sure, but I thought I heard something.

Something faint. *Not* from the door.

Something from *behind* me.

Something like... *a whisper...*

Did you get chills? Because I did.

I tried to make out where it came from, but the more I focused, the more I realized it wasn't just *one* whisper. It was a *bunch* of whispers, all speaking at the same time. I only understood pieces of sentences.

"*...he's not supposed to be...*"

"*...unless he was invited...*"

"*But if he was... what do you think...*"

"*...not supposed to be here...*"

"*...but if... and he sees... then he must...*"

"*...scavengers...*"

I turned my head. "Scavengers?"

And then I heard it. Someone said my name...

"*...Max Cooper...*"

My brain went into "*NOPE!*" mode, and I sprinted to catch up with Beck. You ever sprint somewhere in the dark because you think you're being followed? It was, like, the fastest I had ever run in my life. It felt like my feet weren't even touching the ground. I could probably run a two-minute mile in that hallway if I tried.

I slid to a stop just behind my friend. Beck was still pointing his Holo Pen at random spots in the hall.

"Whoa," Beck said. "What's the matter with you?"

I rested my hands on my knees, breathing heavily to catch my breath. "Voices," I said between heaves. "Whispers. Back by that door."

Beck made a face. "What? You heard someone whisper something to you?"

I nodded like a bobblehead on a bumpy road.

"It was nothing," Beck said. "Prob'ly just some voices from upstairs coming through the air vents. That, or the roaches. I'm sure they've built a thriving city somewhere in the dungeon, but other than that, we're the only ones down here."

I said nothing, still breathing hard out of my dry mouth.

"Look," Beck said, sliding his hand up the wall until something clicked.

The fluorescent lights above our heads flickered to life. What once was dark was now lit up in a blindingly bright white blanket of light.

…say that five times fast.

Blindingly bright white blanket of light.

The hall where I had just about peed my pants was completely empty. Not a single trace that anyone had been there whispering things to me.

"See?" Beck said. "Totally alone."

I stared at the hallway until I was convinced that my friend was right. The whispers weren't from down there. It was the sound of kids talking upstairs. It had to have been, even though I couldn't hear them anymore. I was so freaked that I must've imagined hearing my own name too.

At least, I hoped I imagined it.

"48," Beck said. "What's that number mean?"

"Classroom numbers?" I suggested. "No wait, the numbers down here don't go that high."

"48 feet?" Beck said, thinking aloud. "Steps? Miles? Hand me that thing."

"Uhhhh," I hesitated. If I gave Beck the letter then he'd see that there weren't any other messages to decode. I ignored him. "Maybe it's 48 feet. Let's start there."

Beck grew frustrated, shooting out his hand. "Give it here!" he demanded.

"The clue didn't say anything else!" I said, upset that my friend yelled at me.

"But you might'a missed something! Let someone *smarter* than you take a look."

"Nice burn, dude."

"I feel like you're hiding something from me!"

I could feel sweat beading at the top of my forehead. "I'm not, man. I just know there's nothing else about this riddle."

Beck pushed his lips to the side, glaring at me. "*Fine,*" he said at last. "If you're not gonna show me, then at least look again by yourself. Turn it sideways and upside-down if you have to."

I got far enough away that Beck couldn't see the letter. I unfolded the paper and held it in front of my face, turning it sideways and upside-down like he suggested, like that was gonna help me see any—

"*Dude!*" I said, slapping my forehead. When the letter was sideways, I caught a glimpse of the number 48 that my great-great-granddad had written.

The number 48 chicken-scratched on the ancient paper was written at an awful angle.

"When I decoded this earlier," I explained to Beck, "I quickly wrote down the number 48, but... what if it's *not* 48?"

Beck stared at me. "Um... okay?"

I walked back to my friend and, in my excitement, tapped on Beck's helmet with my knuckles. "Sideways was the answer!"

My friend stepped backward, and his Tenderfoot Shell froze all of a sudden. His little squid tentacles came up from the bottom of his helmet and held the sides of his head, where I think his ears were. "Don't tap the glass, man! It sounds like a little clink out there, but it's like an explosion in here!"

"I'm sorry!" I said, super embarrassed and feeling awful about hurting my friend's ears. "I just got excited."

Do normal squids have ears? I don't think they do, but I'm pretty sure Tendersquids have them. Beck's ears might be really tiny and barely visible, but they're there. I think.

"It's cool," Beck said, slipping his tentacles back into the bottom of his helmet where the controls were. His robot body came back to life.

I folded the letter and held it up between my thumb and first finger. "It looked like Chase wrote the number 48, but what if he just wrote the number 4? The '8' looks all crooked. Almost like—"

"An infinity symbol." Beck knew exactly what I was talking about. That's probably why we were such good friends. He continued, his voice barely a whisper. "And the only things that have infinity symbols at the school are—"

I was the one to finish *his* sentence that time. "The water fountains."

Beck's squid body swirled in his helmet. I liked when he did that because it meant he was seriously excited about something. Squids were hard to read unless they swirled around with happiness.

"That's why the end of the clue says '*cheers*,' isn't it?" Beck said. "Because it was his way of telling us to look for something we drink! You totally put that together, dude! You're a genius!"

I stared at Beck, wondering if I should take credit for that or not because I wouldn't have looked at the letter differently if he hadn't said it. I went with my gut.

"Yup," I said, pretty sure my face had no expression whatsoever. "I totally nailed it, huh?"

Beck laughed. "You're a liar!" he said. "But I don't even care 'cause we're getting closer to the prize!"

I took the lead, shining my Holo Pen down the open and dark path in front of us, ready for whatever the dungeon had to offer.

14

The dungeon. 10:15 AM.

Like, five minutes later, Beck and I were jogging down a different hallway, trying to figure out which water fountain the clue was talking about. The number "4" was before the infinity symbol, so I figured it must've been the fourth water fountain down there.

Our only problem was that we didn't know which one Chase counted as number four.

The other problem, which might've been a bigger one than the first, was that we could only find *three* water fountains.

There was the one back at the beginning of the dungeon, where the wall had been built to seal it off from the rest of the school.

The second was at the end of the first hallway, where the restrooms were.

And the third was by the elevators that didn't work anymore, tucked away in the corner.

We checked all the water fountains for whatever treasure my great-great-grandad had hidden, but none of them budged, not even a little bit.

"Welp," Beck said. "Back to zero."

"There's not another one down here?" I said. "I can't believe that. There *has* to be."

Beck shook his head. "Let's stop wasting time with that idea," he said. "Maybe we interpreted the whole thing wrong."

I sighed, leaning against the wall and shining my Holo Pen back at the letter. "So we're in the dungeon. At least we know we're *in* the right place."

"So the number four," Beck said, "plus an infinity symbol. *Or* it's just the number forty-eight – We can't say it's *not* that if we're starting over."

"But the more I look at the riddle," I said, drawing an infinity symbol in the air with the light from my Holo Pen. "The more I can only see the infinity symbol."

"What if the number four doesn't mean the *fourth* water fountain?" Beck suggested. "What if it means, like…" Beck thought for a moment, but couldn't come up with anything clever. "*Something!*" he said, frustrated.

"We checked every part of the dungeon?" I asked.

Beck nodded. "Every hallway, at least. We didn't check any rooms or anything, but why would anyone put a water fountain in a classroom?"

"Water fountains are *always* by the bathrooms," I said. "We checked *all* the bathrooms down here."

69

I slid my back down the wall until I was sitting on the cold floor. I waved my Holo Pen at the empty lockers, imagining the hallway packed with students a hundred years ago.

My own family had walked through the dungeon before, I was sure of that. My great-great-grandpa Chase, my great-grandpa whose name I didn't know, my grandpa Logan, and my own dad Juju.

Uh… yeah, my dad's name was Juju. It was the most popular Boy's name around the time he was born. At least that what my Grandpa Logan said, though I've never known a single other person with the name Juju.

Five generations of Coopers have been to Buchanan School. I knew that because our family hadn't moved from the area in the last hundred years. I had cousins and second-cousins and aunts and uncles and great-aunts and great uncles and step-cousins and step-aunts and blah blah blah…

Let's just say my family was large.

I even had an uncle who played the cymbals. He was that dude who stood at the back of the orchestra, waiting for his moment to shine, and when his moment came, *everyone* heard it.

He even took the whole family to the place where he practiced with the rest of the orchestra. They sometimes performed music by Mozart or Beethoven and sometimes played music in the pit for musicals.

It was cool to see where they played. In all the pictures I'd ever seen, he and fifty other people were dressed in fancy tuxes and dresses. But their practice space was just a large room with chairs and music stands set up in a circle.

There was nothing fancy about their practice room. Just a big empty space with fabric walls and a shiny floor.

The whole thing looked exactly like our orchestra room on the third floor of Buchanan School. Even the bathroom at the back of the room was in the same place…

My brain tickled, like it was trying to… yeah, I think it was trying to tell me something.

The orchestra room on the third floor of the school looked just like the orchestra room where my uncle practiced… and both had their own bathrooms…

I was sure that I had passed the old orchestra room when we first got in the basement. If it was anything like the other two I was thinking about, it might've had a bathroom of its own, and normally where there's a bathroom... a drinking fountain wasn't too far away.

I looked at Beck, who was standing over me. Apparently he had been trying to get my attention, but I had been too distracted to notice.

"Dude, you okay?" he asked. "You need air or something? I can't tell 'cause I'm living in this glass mask filled with water, but... are the oxygen levels alright out there?"

I sat up. "We didn't check *all* the bathrooms," I said.

"Pretty sure we did," Beck said.

I didn't even bother explaining. Instead, I bounced to my feet and started jogging back to the orchestra room.

Beck shouted something at me, but I had no idea what. I was too excited about finding that fourth water fountain.

If I was right, then whatever we were looking for was almost within reach.

I was sprinting so fast that I felt like I was running on clouds. The adventure and excitement that I always wanted had been delivered to me by my great-great-grandad, and I was about to find whatever treasure he had hidden for me.

I wish I had known him. He probably had the coolest life filled with all kinds of exciting thrills and spills – living without a care in the world.

He probably never had a single problem. A kid like him was probably the most popular kid in the school with a bajillion friends and zero enemies.

Whatever treasure I was about to find was sure to be awesome – it was probably gonna be something so crazy that it would change my life forever.

15

The dungeon. 10:20 AM.

I stared at the fourth and final water fountain.

I was right.

It *was* in the orchestra room.

And on the wall behind the fountain was a giant word painted in black that said "FOUR." A few feet down was the word "THREE."

"TWO" and "ONE" were on another wall.

Orchestras had four sections – strings, woodwind, brass, and percussion. The walls told students where to sit during practice. I know this because I played cello in fourth grade for a week, and then quit. The giant "FOUR" was where the percussion kids were supposed to sit. A bathroom with a water fountain was behind their chairs.

I stepped up to the fountain, feeling stupid because I had peeked into the orchestra room when Beck and I first got into the dungeon, but didn't point my Holo Pen at the wall. I would've seen the ginormous numbers if I had.

The fountain even had the little infinity logo staring me right in the face.

Beck pressed the knob at the top to get water to shoot from the spigot. And y'know what? It worked.

"Huh," Beck grunted. "Look at that."

"Do you drink water?" I asked, surprised that I didn't know. "If squids swim in water all day long, then do you, like, breath it? Or drink it? Or what?" I paused, feeling like my brain was about to spill out a bunch of questions I hadn't thought of until that very second. "Do you breath air? Like, oxygen? Do you get it from the water you drink? Or wait... the water you breath? Lungs? Do you have lungs? Can you drown in air the way humans drown in water? *How do you work?*"

"That's a question for your parents," Beck joked, putting his hands around the water fountain. He pulled gently, but nothing happened.

I pressed my face against the wall to see what was behind the water fountain, but it was too dark even when I pointed my Holo Pen at it.

There wasn't anything different about the fountain. It looked like the other three in the dungeon, and there wasn't any clear opening that my great-great-grandad could've hid his treasure in.

It looked like a four-foot tall rusty box with a spigot on top.

"This has *got* to be it," I said, looking at the giant "FOUR" as it loomed over us. "Pull harder."

"I can't," Beck said, letting go of the fountain. "This Tenderfoot Shell is only allowed so much power."

"Really?" I asked.

"Yup," Beck said. "Otherwise these suits would be superpowered monster rigs. Think about it. I'm *wearing* a robotic exoskeleton. Without restrictions, this thing could rip a tree right out of the ground."

"Yikes," I said.

"I know, right?" Beck said. "You'll have to help me if we wanna move the water fountain."

Setting my great-great-grandad's letter on the floor next to me, I brushed off my hands like they were dusty and then wrapped my fingers around the back edges of the fountain.

Beck pressed his robot fingers into the top. "One… two…" Beck said. "*Three!*"

Both of us pulled on the metal box at the same time, which made it scoot slightly.

It didn't move far, but it was enough for me to see that the back of the fountain wasn't covered. All we had to do was get it out another inch or two and I could slip my hand behind it.

"Keep pulling," I grunted, feeling the fountain scoot a bit farther.

Metal scraped on the floor, screaming in the dead silent dungeon. It echoed down the hall outside the orchestra room doors.

"Just a little…" I said, and then stopped when I saw it.

At the very bottom of the fountain was a gritty-looking plastic bag that had been folded neatly and tucked away.

"I see it!" I said, pulling harder. "I just need another inch so I can get my fingers down there!"

Beck pressed his robotic fingers between the wall and the fountain and wedged the rest of his hand into the space, giving me the opening I needed.

I slid my hand down the side and grabbed the little plastic bag.

When I took the bag out, Beck let the fountain go. It slammed back, again echoing metal screams off the walls.

"What's in it?" Beck asked.

"It's kinda heavy," I said, setting the plastic bag down gently and unfolding the tiny package as carefully as I could. I wasn't sure what was in it, but I didn't want to test whether it could survive some rough handling after a hundred years under a rusty water fountain.

I removed everything from the inside of the plastic bag. Beck and I stared, dumbfounded at what we had found.

There was a tiny slip of paper prob'ly as old as the letter from the time capsule. Written on it was "B-LO G42."

Next to the paper was a small black box with a white sticker on the front of it. The box was about half the size of a deck of cards. On the sticker were the words, "*NOT* NINJA SECRETS."

The last thing from the bag was a golden key.

That was it.

I was a little discouraged, but Beck was excited.

He snatched my great-great-grandad's letter out of my back pocket. "This thing is like a treasure map!" he said, waving it around. "I bet there are all *kinds* of secrets on here! Secrets that lead to other hidden things in the school!"

I grabbed at the letter in Beck's hand and tried to take it back, but his grip was fierce. "C'mon, man! Give it here!"

Immediately, Beck let go, which sent me plopping onto the floor.

Beck took a knee and scooped up the black box and piece of paper that were still on the floor. He didn't even say he was sorry for making me fall on my butt.

"What do you think that is?" I asked, getting back on my feet.

"Looks like some sort of old tech," Beck said. "Do you recognize it at all?"

Beck dropped the box into my hand. It was tiny and made of plastic. The top looked like it opened up, but I didn't want to force it just in case it was weak. "No idea," I said. "But you're right. It looks like some kind of old-fashioned tech… What're we supposed to do with this?"

Beck fell silent for a moment, studying the box in my hand. And then, like a light bulb switched on in his head, he looked up at me with clear eyes. "You know who we should take this to?"

I shook my head.

"Patrick Scott," Beck said like I was supposed to know who that was.

"Who's Patrick Scott?"

"You don't know Patrick? Super genius? Practically lives in the library? Eleven-year-old taking college level courses at Buchanan because he's more comfortable here than at a real college?"

I smiled, still unsure who Beck was talking about.

"He's cool!" Beck said. "He's kind of a loner, so he'll love the company. He's a braniac, and a history buff. If anyone will know what that little box is, it's him."

Beck snatched the black box out of my hand and jogged back through the orchestra room doors.

I'd never met Patrick before, but if Beck thought he was cool, then it meant that he was cool.

As I turned to follow Beck, I heard them again – the same whispers that I heard before, but this time they sounded closer. They actually sounded like they were *in* the room with me.

I spun around, shining my Holo Pen over every inch of the room until I was certain I was alone. I didn't know what was scarier to me – the fact that I couldn't find where the whispers were coming from or the fact that I was completely alone in that dark room.

"Max!" Beck shouted from down the hall.

I about jumped outta my skin, scared half to death.

"It's the roaches," I said quietly. "That's all it is…"

But I wasn't about to test the idea that roaches had mutated and learned to talk. I didn't waste another second and was out the door as fast as my scrawny little legs could take me.

16

The library. 10:45 AM.

Several minutes later, Beck held the door to the library open.

Patrick was supposed to be in one of the rooms near the back, working on his college courses.

Beck mentioned that Patrick was a super genius. I'm not sure exactly what makes someone a super genius, but whatever it was, Patrick had it.

On the way outta the dungeon, Beck gave me the shortened story of Patrick's life.

Patrick started talking at eight months, when he looked up at his mom and asked her for something to eat *other* than mushed up bananas and prunes.

At two years old, he was reading at a sixth grade level.

At five years old, he could speak seven different languages.

Finished high school *with* specialized honors in mathematics as a nine-year-old.

Earned the highest SAT score in the city with a perfect 800 in math.

And now he was working on getting his PHD in quantum mechanics/physics by fifteen years old.

You know how smart that is? That's so smart that I didn't even understand *half* the stuff up there!

But with all that, Patrick was still an eleven-year-old. If he were a normal student, he'd be in the sixth grade at Buchanan School with everyone else his age, but he was *not* a normal student.

His parents didn't want him to attend college with a bunch of adults because he was still a kid, which was why he was allowed to study and do his work in the library at

Buchanan School. It was also the reason why I didn't know who he was.

Patrick was *at* Buchanan but didn't *go* to Buchanan.

Beck and I walked right past the librarian behind her desk. She was so busy reading something on her computer that she didn't even notice us.

"No way," she whispered to herself. "*Those* two are dating now? Holy buckets of cabbage, Debbie's gonna blow a gasket when she hears about this…"

At the back of the library, Beck looked both ways down each aisle and then nodded. "Oh, right. He's back here."

The corner of the library was where Patrick had his own workspace. His door was shut, but the wall was made of glass so we could see inside.

The room wasn't small, but it was cramped because of all the stacks of books and papers he had inside. It didn't surprise me to see that he handwrote his notes instead of using a Holo Pen. There was an art and beauty to the way real paper looked when there was a ton of it.

Different machine parts were scattered throughout the room. I couldn't make any sense out of the way he organized things, but maybe that was just how his brain worked.

Beck and I stood outside the glass wall, trying to look over the book stacks.

"Is he even in there?" I asked, pressing my nose against the glass.

"I'unno," Beck said, knocking gently on the wooden door to Patrick's room.

Almost as if Patrick had been waiting for us, his door swung wide open, and he leaned his body out, studying Beck and me.

I was shocked. Patrick didn't look the way I thought he would. I was expecting some pale, pimply-faced, short and scrawny, glasses-wearing, nasally-voiced kid who avoided eye contact.

Patrick was *not* that.

In fact, he was the opposite. He was tall, dark, and big-boned with a deep voice – not *deep* deep, like a grown-up, but deep for an eleven-year-old. The only odd thing about him? He was wearing a heavy set of metallic goggles, which gave him bug eyes.

You hear stories of the smart kids getting picked on at school. But it was clear that *nobody* picked on Patrick since he could probably squash 'em like a gnat.

A high-pitched voice came from the inside of the room from behind Patrick. "*Who is it?*"

Patrick sighed, turning slightly. "I don't know yet, dude."

"Is it my pizza? I ordered a pizza!"

"Pizza? You know you shouldn't be eating!" Patrick said.

Beck and I looked at each other. Neither one of us were sure what to do.

"I knooow," the voice said. "But I loooove the way pizza smells!"

"The way you *think* it smells," Patrick sighed.

"Just—is it my pizza or what?"

Patrick turned to us. "You guys got pizza?"

Beck and I shook our heads at the same time.

Patrick leaned back and spoke loudly. "It's *not* your pizza."

"Awwwwww," the voice said with a softly disappointed tone, which escalated until it was frustrated. "Awwwwwrrrraaaaaagh!"

I heard a tiny fist punch something. And then I heard it again. And again, and again, until I was sure there was a small barrage of fists getting thrown all over the place.

"*Really?*" Patrick said.

It was one of the most uncomfortable, strangest things I had ever seen. My brain wasn't sure what to do with it.

"What's happening?" I whispered to Beck. "We're about to die, aren't we?"

Beck shrugged his shoulders, trying to see past Patrick.

The super genius stretched and stood taller so Beck couldn't see anything in the room.

"Hey, dude!" Beck said, putting his hand on Patrick's shoulder.

The way that Beck spoke to the super genius made me think they were old buds or something, but that's not how it was either.

Patrick pushed Beck's robotic hand off his shoulder. "Who're you?"

"It's me!" my best friend said. "Beck! We met that one time at the school picnic! Remember? I asked if you wanted a hotdog, and you blinked at me and then walked away!"

"Lotsa people offerin' hotdogs that day," Patrick said. "Can't expect me to remember every one of 'em."

"Riiiiight," Beck said, trailing off. "But I was prob'ly the only squid who offered you one."

"Maybe. Maybe not."

"Not alotta squids at Buchanan."

"There's not?"

"Oh, right. You're not actually a student here. Um…"

"Should that matter? You'd think I'd remember a Tendersquid offering me a hotdog. That's not the kind of thing that happens everyday."

"I know, right? That's what I'm saying! I offered you a hotdog! I'm a Tendersquid! A *squid*. Inside a *robot*. I offered you a *hotdog*. And you don't remember it?"

"That didn't happen," Patrick said, all serious and stuff.

"Yes, it—wait…" Beck's eyes stared off. "You're right. I never did that. I *wanted* to do it, but didn't. I even went through the scenario in my head where you rejected the hotdog and walked away. Whoops. Uh… sorry."

Patrick stared at the two of us. We must've looked just as strange to him as he did to us. "I have work to do," Patrick said. "And you're wasting my time."

"Fair enough," Beck said. "Then let's start over… my name is—"

Patrick slammed his door shut before Beck could even finish his sentence.

"*Nope!*" Patrick's voice said through the heavy wooden door.

I couldn't help but laugh. "That went well!"

17

Patrick's workspace. 10:50 AM.

"That dude just slammed the door in my face," Beck said, annoyed.

"I know," I said. "I was right next to you when it happened, like, five seconds ago. Hey, remember that time when Patrick slammed the door in your face?" I fake chuckled. "Good times…"

Beck knocked loudly on Patrick's door. The "*CLUNK*" sound of his metal fist against the heavy wood traveled through the library.

"Not interested," Patrick said from behind the door.

"Come on, man!" Beck said, almost as if he were trying to be kind, but that all went out the window when he shouted. "*Open the flippin' door!*"

Through the glass, we could see the lights switch off inside the room. And heard the "*shhhhhhhh*" sound he made to whoever else was with him.

"Seriously?" I said. "You're gonna just pretend you're not home?"

The person with the high-pitched voice spoke loudly enough that we could hear him through the glass. "I think they know we're here."

"Just ignore them," Patrick said. "They'll go away."

The other person paused. "But what if it's the pizza I ordered?"

Beck looked at me with a smile, and then he pounded on the door once more. "Pizza guy! Someone in there order a pizza?"

The high-pitched voice squealed joyfully.

"No, wait!" Patrick said. "You can't unplug yet!"

"Can't unplug?" I repeated to Beck.

The light in Patrick's room switched back on, and the door pulled open. Patrick was standing there wearing his "annoyed" face.

"*What* do you guys want?" Patrick said.

I held the black box Beck and I had found in the dungeon up to Patrick's face. "All we need is for you to tell us what this is."

After studying the box for a second, he spoke. "Where'd you get that?"

"In the dungeon," I said. "Er... um... I mean, the basement."

"I know what the dungeon is," Patrick said, stepping aside. "Come in."

"Nice," Beck said, patting my back as I walked through the door.

The inside of Patrick's room looked pretty much the way I thought it'd look. I mean, I could see that it was a mess through the glass wall, but that was only the tip of the iceberg.

The floor had a single path that led from the door to a desk at the back. The path was made from worn down textbooks and thick stacks of paper. Between a few of the towers of books was an empty pizza box or two.

And the room smelled like cheese.

"Gross," I said.

"Don't be like that," Patrick said. "Your bedroom prob'ly looks the same."

"But this isn't your bedroom," Beck said.

"Touché," Patrick said as he took the lead, carefully stepping down the winding path of junk.

Whoever Patrick was talking to earlier wasn't in the room with us. At least not that I could see.

As cluttered and messy as it seemed, there were still some pretty cool things in there. Almost everywhere I looked was some kind of machine buzzing and clicking and moving on its own.

Tiny little robots the size of softballs jumped back and forth across the stacked piles of paper, stamping different symbols on each stack before moving onto the next one.

Across the room was a large machine, about the size of a chair, humming softly, shooting little beams of red light at a spot beneath it. I didn't know what it was doing, but it looked pretty sweet.

Patrick had two desks in the room. I didn't notice the second one until we were closer to it because it had a bunch of random machinery parts laying on top of it.

And right next to me was a small metal button, about the size of a quarter, that was *floating* in the air, spinning slowly and glowing. The button sizzled and then zapped every few seconds.

Several of the same buttons were laying on the box under it, but they weren't floating *or* glowing. There had to be about thirty of them.

My brain was like, "*Don't touch it, don't touch it, don't touch it, don't touch it!*"

I touched it.

The button zapped, stinging my finger.

I flinched, knocking stacks of paper to the ground.

Patrick spun around. "*Don't touch that! Do you realize what you could've done?*"

"Um... no." I said, putting my finger in my mouth to try to stop the burn.

Patrick made his way back over to me, carefully pinching the top of the floating button. "This is a teleporter I've been working on. I call it a tele-pin, y'know, 'cause it looks like a pin."

Teleporters *did* exist, but there were only, like, *five* of them in the whole world. And one of those five was definitely *not* in some eleven-year-old kid's workshop.

Plus a *real* teleporter was the size of a school bus, and the thing Patrick was holding in his hand was the size of a quarter. The kid was just trying to sound cool.

"You coulda zapped your hand off," Patrick said, placing the glowing button on top of another stack of papers – not exactly a safer place for it.

"Sure," I said, examining my finger. "You've built a working teleporter that you keep here in your oversized locker."

"I did," Patrick said matter-of-factly. "And it's called a tele-pin."

"Yeah?" Beck said. "So teleport me! Show us how it works!"

Patrick shook his head. "I haven't been able to make it teleport anything larger than a basketball. That and..."

"Annnd?" Beck said slowly.

"I don't know where the things I teleport end up," Patrick said, embarrassed.

I let out a laugh. "So you're saying you can make things disappear, but have no idea where they reappear?"

Patrick nodded, staring at the glowing button.

I couldn't believe what I was hearing. "Are you *nuts?!* For all you know you're vaporizing the things you're supposed to be teleporting! Oh, man," I said, fully realizing how awful Patrick's invention really was. "Have you tried that thing on anything living yet?"

Patrick ignored me as he continued walking. I didn't even want to know why he didn't answer my question.

I had to step over a small pile of fruit he kept in a torn paper bag on the floor. If I had to guess, I'd say it was for a snack healthier than pizza. But then I'd ask you why you were making me guess that in the first place.

Besides, the fruit couldn't have been that fresh – there were little flies buzzing all around the bag.

At the desk against the back wall, Patrick took a seat and spun around. "Hand me that cassette."

"Hmm? The what now?" I said.

"The black box you showed me at the door. It's called a cassette," Patrick sighed. "You guys don't know what a cassette is?"

Beck looked at me, confused.

"I know what a cassette is," I said, trying my best to play it cool. "But, like, *you* should tell *me* what you think it is so *I* know if *you* know."

Patrick leaned back in his chair. "Okaaay," he said with a mocking tone. "Why don't you just give it to me so I can explain."

I set the black cassette in Patrick's hand, but before he could say anything else, a SPUD appeared in the aisle right behind us. My heart sunk when I saw it because I knew it meant we were busted, probably for going into the dungeon.

"You two have a lot of explaining to do," the SPUD said.

Great.

Game over.

And just when things were getting interesting.

18

I put both of my hands in the air, surrendering to the SPUD that caught us.

"You're not getting robbed," Beck said.

The SPUD took a step toward me, which made me take one step back. And then he did it again. And then again. It looked like we were dancing.

The robot was wearing a green stocking cap on top of his round head, which was *kind* of adorable. And the SPUD's eyes weren't blue like the other SPUDs. This SPUD had green eyes, the same color as the stocking cap.

"You two have a lot of explaining to do," the SPUD repeated.

"I know," I said. "It was all my fault. I got this stupid letter this morning, and then I found out it was from someone in my family, and my curiosity got the better of me, and I—"

The SPUD cut me off. "You *said* you were delivering the *pizza* I ordered. Explain the lack pizza in your hands!"

I fumbled over my words. "Uh, I, uh… what? Pizza?"

"Mochi!" Patrick said. "For the last time, you can't even *eat* pizza so stop asking for it!"

"Mochi?" Beck repeated.

The SPUD snapped to attention with his arms at his sides. "*Mochi*: a Japanese rice cake!"

The screen on the SPUD's face flickered, and then he was smiling. Up until that moment, I had never seen a SPUD smile.

"But you're a SPUD," I said.

"I am Mochi," the small robot said, still wearing a cheesy smile.

Patrick leaned forward. "Mochi," he said. "You're gonna get me into a ton of trouble if you keep ordering pizzas like that."

Mochi frowned, looking at Patrick.

"I thought I said you couldn't unplug yet," Patrick said.

"I finished charging," Mochi replied, scooting his foot on the floor like a kid in trouble.

Patrick sighed. "Guys, this is my friend Mochi. Mochi, this is Max and Beck."

The little robot flung his arm up at me. "Hi!" he said, excited.

Mochi was so cute that I didn't even hesitate to shake his hand. "Wow," I said. "So this is a SPUD?"

"Built from SPUD parts, yes," Patrick said, "but *not* a SPUD. He's not connected to the SPUD mainframe so he's on his own."

"How'd you manage that?" Beck said. "Blocking the mainframe from him?"

"It was pretty easy. I changed his programming," Patrick said. "This way, Mochi learns things on his own and at his own speed, *without* the mainframe. He has his own mind – his own personality. He'll grow from his own experiences."

"No way," Beck said. "This guy has his own brain?"

Patrick nodded with a big smile. "Not a *real* brain, but that's why he's kind of weird. He's a toddler. Had to start him as a baby if the program was gonna work."

"I am a unique *snoooooowflake*," Mochi whispered, pushing his lips together, and then followed it with a silent explosion sound effect. "Ka-pssssshhhhhhhhhhh... snowflake war."

"Gnarly," I said.

"Mochi's not connected to the mainframe, but he *is* connected to my battle station," Patrick continued, pointing at the computer screen on his desk. "So in case there *is* something he needs to know, I can upload it to him in an instant."

Beck stared at Mochi, awestruck by the strange robot. "How'd you get Principal Green to let you make him?"

Patrick took a breath. "She kinda doesn't know about him. In fact, nobody does. I'd probably get in trouble if anyone found out about him."

Beck and I looked at each other.

Patrick held the cassette in the palm of his hands. "This thing is an *antique*," he said. "Where'd you find it?"

I started to explain, but Beck interrupted me.

"Can you just tell us what it is?" he asked. "Doesn't matter *where* we got it."

"It's an old cassette tape," Patrick said, using tweezers to pry open the top. "Looks like the kind that has video on it."

"Do you have something that'll read it?" I asked.

"You mean 'play' it," Patrick said, squinting at the black band inside the cassette. "Yeah, I have a video player somewhere in this room. It's as old as the hills, but it'll do the trick."

"Nice," I said, scanning the cluttered office with my eyes. "Where is it?"

"Well," Patrick said quietly, scraping the black band gently. "Before any of that, I'm gonna have to clean this thing up. It's super old and brittle. If we put it in the video player right now, it'll probably crack apart."

"Yeah, we don't want that."

"If you guys can give me about an hour, I should have it ready by then. I'll even convert it so it's digital."

"An hour?" I said to Beck.

"It'll give us time to figure out the key and the second message from the water fountain," Beck whispered. "Remember? B-LO G42?"

I had completely forgotten about the rest of the treasure we found in the dungeon.

"Cool," I said, and then turned back to Patrick. "What do we owe you?"

"*Monies*," Mochi spouted. "*All* your monies."

"*Nothing*," Patrick said.

Mochi's face turned to a frown. "Awww."

Patrick lifted his goggles off his eyes. "This junk is fun for me. But… just don't tell anyone about Mochi, and we're good."

"Deal," I said. "We'll be back in a bit."

I'm not sure Patrick even heard me because he didn't say anything. He was too busy cleaning the cassette.

Part of me worried about leaving such an ancient treasure with someone I just met, and no matter how hard I tried, I couldn't shake the feeling.

It was the same feeling I got when something bad was about to happen. It was a feeling deep in my gut, like butterflies were waging war inside my stomach. It was like someone shook up a soda can, and I was just waiting for it to pop.

Something bad was coming... I just didn't know what.
Nine out of ten times, my gut feeling was wrong.
But that one time when it was right?
Man... was it right.

19

The library. 11:25 AM.

Beck and I sat at a table near the library exit. The librarian up front was still hypnotized by her computer screen, making comments about what celebrities were dating or broken up. Around the room were a few other students sitting at desks watching hologram lessons from their Holo Pens.

"This is the best day ever," Beck said. "I'm so pumped that we've finally gotten a day that's different than the rest. Seriously? I *might* be a little *overexcited*. I *might* have to change the water in my helmet."

"I know, right?" I said, showing him my forearms. "I got goosebumps! Just like Lexi!"

Beck leaned closer. "So what's next in that letter?"

"I'm not sure," I paused, and then took the slip of paper we found with the cassette out of my pocket. "We should figure out what this means first."

Beck nodded. "Yeah, you're right," he said. "Let's do that one first."

"Well, not *first*," I said, but I didn't want Beck to lose interest in the letter he thought had more to it than it did, so I said, "I'll probably spend the rest of the time until lunch decoding as much of this letter as possible. Lotsa good stuff on here, I think."

I don't know why I was stretching the truth even farther. I had no end-game. No way to cover for the fact that there *weren't* other codes to crack.

"Shouldn't be hard," I said. "I already know most of the code. But hopefully I can figure out this B-LO G42 thing too. When I find it, I'll let you know what it is!"

"No!" Beck growled as he angled his squid body downward so that his eyes were near the neck. "You *can't* do it alone! That's such a lame wad thing to do! I need to be there too! You need me to even do it, dude!"

I knew Beck wanted to be in on the excitement, but I didn't know he wanted it *that* bad. "Alright, man, sorry. I'll wait until—"

"You couldn't find your own underwear if you were wearing them," Beck continued, completely ignoring me.

"Okay, that happened *one time*, and you swore you'd never bring it up!"

"You'd better not leave me behind on this. I'll be so miffed if you do."

I laughed, because I didn't know what to say. "Dude, listen," I said, putting my hand on Beck's robotic shoulder. I wondered if he could even feel it. "I won't do this without you, alright? We're in this together. Bro-punch?"

Beck's squid body floated in his glass helmet for a moment. And then he drifted back to his normal position with a tiny smile on his face. "Bro-punch," he said.

I jabbed his robotic shoulder with my fist. And then he did the same thing to me, except his sent me flying off my chair.

Rolling to the floor, I shot my hands out to stop myself, but the librarian's desk did a better job of doing it than I could.

Beck came running over to me, both hands out, his voice heavy with embarrassment. "I'm sorry, I'm sorry, I'm sorry!"

I sat against the librarian's desk, who by the way, didn't even look up from whatever online article she was reading.

"It's cool," I laughed.

"Dude, I'm *so* sorry," Beck said. "This shell can be a lot stronger than I remember sometimes."

"Weird," I said. "I thought you said those things were only allowed so much power."

Beck paused. "Uh, yeah. Maybe I hit you just right. Like, on the funny bone in your shoulder."

"Humans don't have funny bones in their shoulders," I said.

Beck shrugged. "I'unno then," he said. And then he flipped a panel open on his wrist. I thought he was going to check the safety settings, but he didn't. He was looking at the time. "So we've got about ten minutes 'till lunch. Meet in the lobby in about fifteen? I've got some stuff I have to do."

"What do you have to do?"

Beck laughed, holding his hand out to me. "Change the water in my helmet."

"Alright," I said, taking Beck's hand. "Fifteen minutes. I'll be there."

Beck left the library to do whatever he had to do. Since I had nothing of my own planned, I figured that was the best time to go to the bathroom. If the next clue was going to take us into some creepy place, I'd rather not do it with a full bladder.

That, and my mom always warned me about getting into an accident while wearing dirty underwear. I don't know – if I got into an accident, I think I'd have more important things to worry about than dirty underwear.

Or… what if getting into an accident was the thing that *caused* the underwear to get dirty? *Then* what, I ask you? *Then* what?

20

The lobby during lunch. 11:40 AM.

After the bell rang, I stepped into the lobby to wait for Beck in the nook.

There were a few seconds of peaceful silence that I loved whenever I was alone in any part of the school. It always felt like kind of a dream.

Before anyone else was out there, the metal door next to the elevator swung open and out stepped a herd of SPUDs. There were five of them marching in a line, which was weird because I'd never seen more than two SPUDs together at a time.

The students spilling into the lobby took my mind off the little robots. Honestly, I didn't really care about the SPUDs. Tenderfoot Industries was probably testing a whole batch of them at the same time.

Almost all at once, the hallways were packed with kids desperately seeking air after being held up tiny classrooms that *sorta* felt like prison cells with no bars. Some of them even squinted their eyes as they walked into the lobby, like they hadn't seen the sun for ages.

Kids can be dramatic sometimes.

"Max Cooper," Bloom said, stepping out from the flowing river of students. "S'up, ninja?"

"Ninja?"

"Yeah, I dunno. I said it before thinking. There's something different about you today… something…" she said, trying to think of a word.

"Something ninja?"

"No… " she said. "The opposite of that. Something…"

"Samurai!" I said, supes proud. "There's something *samurai* about me today!"

97

Bloom made a face. "Nooooooo!" she said. "There's something… *goofy* about you today. Like, you've had a stupid grin on your face all morning. What gives?"

"Yeah," Lexi said, appearing just as suddenly as Bloom had. "What gives?"

"What? I can't smile?" I said, trying to hide my smile, but failing miserably. Trying to keep from doing it only made it bigger.

"What're you hiding?" Bloom said, kicking my shoe gently. "I know you, Maximilian. You're a knob when it comes to keeping secrets, so spill 'em. Now."

"You're real name is Maximilian?" Lexi blurted out, covering her mouth because she accidentally spit everywhere. "Whoops."

"Hey, thanks, Bloom!" I said, embarrassed.

"Why don't you tell her your middle name?" Bloom said with a devious grin. "Or *I* will."

"Ugh," I groaned. "C'mon…"

"Then tell us what you're hiding behind that creepy grin of yours," Bloom said.

"Fine," I said. My middle name was bad, but it wasn't *that* bad. It wasn't like my middle name was, like, Francis or anything…

My apologies to anyone named Francis.

Not for *saying* it was a bad name.

But *because* it's a bad name.

Sorry.

"This is about that letter, isn't it?" Bloom said.

"What happened?" Lexi spoke faster as she got excited. "Did you and Beck go into the dungeon? What was down there? What was it like? Were there dead bodies? There were dead bodies, weren't there? Oh man, don't tell me if there were dead bodies! But were there dead bodies?"

My smile stretched from ear to ear. "We *did* go there. There *weren't* any dead bodies. It *was* empty. It *was* dark. It *was* scary, but… we *found* what we were looking for."

"Eeep!" Lexi squealed. "What was it?"

"It wasn't another clue, was it?" Bloom said sarcastically. "Hate when that happens."

I paused. "Actually, yeah, it was another clue."

"Oh, um…" Bloom hummed and then faked a laugh. "I mean… *yay!* So great."

"So there was a slip of paper that said 'B-LO G42,' a golden key, and a little black cassette tape," I said.

"What's a cassette tape?" Bloom asked, wrinkling her nose.

"Right?" I said. "And Patrick thought it was lame that I didn't know!"

"What?" Lexi said. "Who's Patrick?"

"Okay," I said. "So there was a cassette tape that we found. Beck said that a kid named Patrick would probably know what it was. Patrick's the kid in the library who goes to school here, but *doesn't* go to school here."

"Oh, the super nerd," Lexi said, snapping her finger. "I mean... the *smart* kid."

"Right," I said. "So Patrick said the cassette tape was how people used to record video, like, a hundred years ago. That means my great-great-gramps prob'ly wanted to show me a video or something."

"You didn't watch it?" Bloom said.

I shook my head. "No. It was too old and dirty. Patrick's cleaning it up right now. Said it'll probably work in about an hour. So, while we're waiting for that, Beck and I are trying to figure out what this key and second message means."

"The key is probably to open a lock," Lexi said.

"Duh-doy," Bloom whispered.

Lexi's eyes shot daggers at Bloom. "But the *lock* is prob'ly where the *message* is gonna take you."

As the two girls argued with each other, I tapped the side of my Holo Pen to check the time. It felt like Beck was forever getting back to the lobby, and when I saw what time it was, I found out I was right.

"Sorry!" Bloom said, smiling at Lexi.

"Me too," Lexi replied. "Let's never fight again, okay?"

"Deal," Bloom said. "We'll only fight if we use our fists."

"No," Lexi said, her face growing pale. "That's not what I—"

"Hey, man," Beck said to me, finally showing up.

"Sorry I'm late. Are you ready to—wait…" he leaned closer to me and whispered. "What are *they* doing here?"

"You're, like, a foot away from us," Bloom sighed. "We can totally hear you."

Beck's eyes darted back and forth between Bloom and me. "Question still stands," he said, and then gasped. "You didn't tell them what we *found*, did you?"

"Uh, yeah," Lexi said, bouncing her head slightly. "He did. So? What do you care?"

My best friend paused, and then answered honestly. "I just wanna make sure Max's letter is protected. If it got in the wrong hands... y'know."

Bloom and Lexi didn't say anything, but their faces told the story of two *very* annoyed girls.

I took the small slip of paper and the golden key from my pocket and set it on the carpet of the step we were all sitting on so everyone could see.

"B-LO G42," Lexi read.

"That key is so old school," Bloom said. "All locks are digital anymore, except for a few random places."

"Random places like where?" I asked.

"Tool sheds," Bloom said. "Tool boxes. Tool kits. Tool tools."

"Okay," I laughed. "But what about *other* than tool things?"

"Certain cabinets," Beck said. "Science lab cabinets."

"Cabinet keys are all bigger than this one," Bloom said. "Besides, whatever Max's great-great-gramps is hiding prob'ly ain't stashed away in a spot that gets opened, like, every single day."

"She's right," I said. "This key is small."

Lexi pointed at the slip of paper. "B-LO G42," she repeated. "I don't know what B-LO stands for, but G42 sounds like the locker numbers in the girl's locker room."

"G42?" I said. "That's weird. The boy's lockers all start with B... aaaaand I'm just now realizing the G stands for 'girl' and the B stands for 'boy.'"

"That *does* look like a locker key," Beck said.

The lockers in the gym were barely ever used, but when someone needed one, they could just grab a key from the coach. The lockers all shared the same key, so all we had to do was remember which one we used.

"B-LO," Lexi said softly. "Below? Below locker G42?"

"This one," Bloom said, pointing at Lexi with the thumb. "She's a smart cookie."

"Okay," I said, standing with the paper and the key. "We got nothin' else so we might as well start there, right?"

Lexi led the way as Beck, Bloom, and I followed closely behind her, determined to get to the end of the hunt. It was so close I could almost smell it…

It smelled like tacos.

Oh, wait, no. That was just the school lunch I was smelling.

And yes, kids in the future still eat tacos.

Future tacos. They're awesome.

Tacos of the fut—nevermind.

21

The girl's locker room. 11:50 AM.

The entrances to the boys' and girls' locker rooms at Buchanan were through the doors in the gymnasium. Or the doors behind the stage in the cafeteria. Or the doors from the hallway *next* to the cafeteria. Or the doors from the outside to the— my point is that there were a million different entrances to either of the locker rooms.

Lexi had taken us through the cafeteria to the ones behind the stage. That was our best bet if we didn't want anyone to see what we were doing.

And don't worry about anyone being in the girl's locker room – it was lunch. Nobody had gym class during lunch.

Once we were up on the stage, we relaxed a little. We had to walk past all the lunch tables filled with kids eating their lunches. I must've been starving because future tacos never smelled so good.

"Hey, can we take a break?" I whispered. "My stomach's empty."

I said I was hungry, but the truth? I had that uneasy feeling in the pit of my gut again. The one that was telling me everything was a bad idea.

"You can eat when you're dead," Beck said.

"*Sleep* when you're dead," Bloom said. "The saying is 'you can *sleep* when you're dead.' How is that not obvious to you? *Eat* when you're dead? Is that a zombie saying?"

"Maybe," Beck huffed.

Lexi pushed some clear plastic containers away from the girl's locker room door. There might've been many entrances to the locker rooms, but that didn't mean all of them got used.

"Wait out here," Lexi said. "I'll go in first to make sure the coast is clear."

102

I nodded.

Lexi slipped through the door and let it shut behind her.

"What do you think it looks like in there?" I asked Beck.

"Beats me," Beck answered. "If it's anything like the boy's locker room, then it ain't pretty."

"Boy's locker room pretty bad?" Bloom asked as she folded her arms and leaned against the wall.

"Yeah," I said. "It's got a smell."

"A smell?" Beck asked. "I wouldn't know. I can't smell anything outside the helmet."

"It's kind of like…" I stopped, trying my best to put my finger on it. "Steamed vegetables or something. Broccoli?"

"Sick," Bloom whispered, disgusted.

"Yeah, I don't even know what broccoli smells like," Beck said.

The door to the girl's locker room swung open, and Lexi smiled at us. "We're good. No one's in here – not even Coach Applegate."

Buchanan School had two coaches – Mr. Applegate and Ms. Applegate. They were related, but not by marriage. They were brother and sister. Mr. Applegate was in charge of the boys' locker room, and Ms. Applegate was in charge of, you guessed it, the girls' locker room.

Bloom waved her hand toward the door. "After you," she said to me.

I went in first with Beck behind me. Bloom took up the last spot.

Once inside, I took a second to soak it all in. I was expecting some kind of beautifully decorated palace filled with chirping birds and green trees. I was waiting for the smell of freshly toasted s'mores to fill my nose holes. I even thought the ceiling would be gone so fluffy clouds could float over my head, giving me peace and happiness.

It wasn't like that at all.

Dark. Cold. Muggy. Those would be the three words I'd use to describe the girl's locker room. It also happened to be the three words I'd use to describe the *boy's* locker room. Well, I might change *cold* to *stanktastic*.

"What d'you think?" Bloom asked as she stepped in front of everyone. She put her arms out and spun in a circle like she was dancing in the rain. "Was it everything you dreamed of?"

"The lockers are pink," Beck said.

"Right," I said. "Ours are green."

"Huh," Bloom said, scratching at her chin. "Guess lockers are always greener on the other side."

Bloom wore a smile as she stared at all three of us, like she was waiting for something.

"Get it?" she asked, still smiling. "Greener on the other side?"

Nobody said anything. She must've made a joke, but none of us got it.

"You guys," she said, rubbing the skin on her forehead.

"G42," Lexi said, walking down one of the pink aisles as she counted quietly. "39, 40, 41… and 42. G42. There you are."

The four of us stood in front of locker G42 and studied it for a moment. The lockers were all stacked two high. One set was on top of another set. G42 was the bottom locker.

We could see the inside of it because the door was ventilated, which meant there were holes in the door to keep everyone's sweaty gym clothes from growing mildew, coming alive, and taking over the world.

Lexi tried pulling the locker open, but it didn't budge.

I held out the key and said nothing. She understood as she took it.

We watched as she slowly slid the key into the locker, hearing every little "clink" sound as it fell into place.

Before doing anything else, she looked at all of us.

Finally, she turned the key to the right. The lock opened without a problem.

"No way," Bloom said.

"Yes," Beck whispered.

I was speechless.

Lexi pulled open the locker to see what Great-Great-Grandfather Chase had hidden for me.

But it was empty.

"Huh," Bloom said. "Kinda thought more would happen."

"B-LO," I said. "*Below* G42."

"Do it," Beck said.

Sliding my fingers along the bottom of the locker, I felt nothing. There wasn't even a chance that something was under the locker because it was as hard as concrete. If there was space under the locker, it would've sounded hollow when I tapped it with my knuckle. It didn't.

I sank in my spot, discouraged, letting my hand slide along the bottom of the locker.

"That can't be it, can it?" Beck said. "Did we just hit a dead end?"

"I think so," I said still sliding my fingers along the bottom edge.

Suddenly I felt the whisper of a draft on the skin of my finger.

"Wait a second," I said, taking my Holo Pen from my ear. I tapped it, switching on the flashlight, and pointed it at the back of the locker.

"What's that?" Lexi asked over my shoulder.

"That's a vent," Beck said.

Beck was right. Against the back wall at the bottom of locker G42 was a vent. If I hadn't bumped it with my knuckle, I wouldn't even have known it was back there.

The vent was small, about the size of a milk jug. I slid my fingers behind it and gently nudged it out until the cover fell off.

"You don't think your gramps hid something back there, do you?" Lexi said.

I shook my head. "You're not makin' this easy," I said super-quietly, like my great-great-grandad could actually hear me.

"Okay, so we go in there, grab the prize, and come back out," Beck said like it was no big deal. "Easy squeezy."

"Uh, do you see the size of that vent?" I said. "There's no way *any* of us is fittin' in that thing."

That's when the craziest thing happened. The neck on Beck's Tenderfoot Shell hummed, and then… Beck's head popped off.

Okay, his head didn't really pop off, but his *helmet* did.

At the bottom of the neck, eight thin robotic legs pushed the helmet away from the rest of the body. Beck was still in his glass helmet filled with water, but it was now climbing down the side of the Tenderfoot Shell.

He looked like some kind of alien spider. With the helmet off the Tenderfoot Shell, Beck's squid body was more visible.

"Kinda feels like I'm seeing you naked," I said. "It's weird."

Beck looked annoyed. "Well, ya just made it weird. Thanks for that."

Paige and Bloom said nothing, but their eyes were glued to Beck.

"Stop staring at me like that!" Beck groaned. "Ugh, forget you guys."

Beck didn't say another word as he climbed into the locker. Two little flashlights on the front of his helmet switched on, and then he disappeared into the small open vent.

"Man," Bloom said. "Wish I was a Tendersquid."

We all stood, watching the black hole where Beck had disappeared.

"So what?" Lexi said. "Do we wait for him to come back or... uh-oh."

Lexi was looking past me, down the row of lockers. The way she said "uh-oh" didn't make me think something *good* was behind me.

My heart stopped when I turned around.

Standing at the end of the aisle were six SPUDs, standing at attention. Twelve glowing blue eyes stared at us.

Busted.

22

The girl's locker room. Noon.

The SPUDs blocked the only way out of the aisle where Lexi,
Bloom, and I were standing. Beck had just taken his head off
and crawled into an air vent behind one of the lockers in the
girl's locker room.

Man, I'm only now hearing how crazy that sounded.
"We're dead," Lexi said. "I knew I was in over my
head."
"You're fine," Bloom said. "It's just some SPUDs. The
worst they'll do is take us down to the principal's office."
"Which will get me grounded for life!" Lexi said,
breathing faster. "Not to mention the *years* of detention I'll
have to serve! I've been there once, but I won't go back, you
guys! I *won't* go back to detention!"
She was almost crying.
Bloom was speechless, watching Lexi have a meltdown.

The SPUDs hadn't moved from their spot. I wasn't sure what they were waiting for, but it was starting to creep me out.

"Okay, fellas," I said, walking forward and tucking my great-great-grandad's letter into my back pocket. "This *isn't* exactly what it looks like."

The SPUDs still said nothing. They all took one step toward me at the same time with such perfect timing that all six of their feet made a single "*CLINK*" sound on the concrete.

"Whoa," Bloom said. "What are they doing? Why aren't they talking?"

And then at that exact moment, the eyes on all six SPUDs blinked and turned from blue to red.

"That can't be good," Bloom said.

"Guys?" I said. "I got a bad feeling about this."

One of the SPUDs parted from the group, marching straight at me. His glowing red eyes in the dark locker room was enough to make it feel like I was in the middle of a bad dream.

I held my hand out like I had *any* kind of authority. "Stop!" I said. "I *order* you to stop right there!"

That should've worked. All SPUDs were programmed to stop when commanded by *anyone.* The SPUD *should've* stopped right where he was, but the creepy little twerp kept comin' at me.

"*Stop!*" I said again, raising my voice. I started backing up, keeping Bloom and Lexi behind me the whole time. But we were down an aisle that had no exit – just a solid brick wall at the end of it.

We were cornered.

The five SPUDs at the other end of the aisle remained perfectly still like little metal statues, watching their robotic comrade as he continued his steady pace toward us.

We used to have this squirrel that lived in our backyard. Every time I saw it playing I'd run out and try to get a better look at it, but the squirrel always dashed away frightened. And then, one day when I ran to see the squirrel, it *didn't* run away. It didn't even move. It just... *stared* at me. I got about two feet away before I realized... *I* had become afraid of the *squirrel*. I turned tail and ran back to my house as fast as I could. When I looked back at the squirrel, it stared me straight in the eye, pointed at me, and then dragged its tiny thumb across its neck. I never saw the squirrel again after that.

The SPUD walking toward me reminded me of that squirrel.

"What's wrong with those things?" Lexi said, worried. "I'm kinda freakin' out here. What if they hurt us?"

Just then I remembered the other rule all SPUDs followed – they were never allowed to touch humans. A sense of relief washed over me because I knew that all the SPUD could do was trap us and nothing else.

"It's cool," I said heroically, glancing over my shoulder at Lexi. "These things can't—"

Before I could even get the rest of my sentence out, the SPUD lunged forward and wrapped its tiny little robot claws around my ankle and squeezed. *HARD.*

My ankle burned like it had been hit with a rock or something.

"What the—" I screamed, kicking my foot out.

The SPUD flew against the wall of lockers and fell apart at his joints, limbs bouncing across the concrete floor back to his freaky little robot friends.

"That thing just touched me!" I said in disbelief, shaking my foot like I was still trying to get the SPUD off me.

"No, it didn't," Bloom said, trying to convince herself none of that was happening. "You just bumped it, right?"

"No, dude!" I said, pulling my pant leg up to show the pinch marks. "Look! It almost broke skin!"

Lexi started waving her hands up and down in front of her, breathing rapidly. "OMG, this isn't happening. This isn't happening! This is bad, you guys!"

Bloom clenched her fists, staring at the end of the aisle. "Pull it together, Lexi," she said. "Because it looks like it's about to get *a lot* worse."

The five other SPUDs had come to life, and they were all walking in our direction.

23

The girl's locker room. 12:05 PM.

Three kids against five robotic school helpers. Well, *four* kids. Beck was still in the air vent under locker G42. His Tenderfoot Shell waited patiently, standing in place at the middle of the dead-end corridor in the girls' locker room.

One of the five SPUDs that had us cornered leapt through the air at Bloom.

The world around me came to a standstill, like someone had paused a game.

I saw Bloom.

I saw the SPUD jumping toward her.

I saw Lexi, huddled up and afraid.

I don't know what happened to me in that split-second, but I reacted before I even had time to think about it.

Balling a tight fist, I threw my hand into the air in front of the SPUD that was going for Bloom. My right forearm scraped against the small robot's face, and then my elbow shot forward, landing a blow right on the SPUD's body, sending his arms and legs flying in all directions.

The body of the SPUD flew back, crashing into one of his friends behind him. Both SPUDs were laying on the cold concrete.

"Three down," Bloom said, striking a pose like she setting up for a free kick in soccer. "Three to go!"

Bloom took two steps and punted one of the last three SPUDs back down the aisle. The body of the robot crashed back and forth between the lockers and fell apart.

"Max!" Lexi screamed.

I spun around in time to catch a SPUD just before he threw a kick to my head. "These things are serious!" I said. "This one just tried to kick me!"

The other SPUD came sprinting toward me while I was trying to keep his friend from hitting my face. It was like babysitting two really naughty robot babies!

The SPUD on the floor launched off the concrete and shot his foot out, like it was a ninja or something.

I moved to block the kick with my shoulder, but I was too late and instead, blocked it with my face.

The metal foot on the SPUD was maybe three or four inches long, but it still felt like I had been hit with a baseball bat.

"Ow!" I screamed, holding the little robot brat. "That's my favorite face!"

Dropping the wiggling SPUD to the floor, I stumbled backward and banged my head against the pink metal lockers. My body flopped to the floor like a ragdoll.

When I looked up, both of the SPUDs were sailing through the air with all four of their fists pointed at me. I flinched, expecting the worst.

But right before the SPUDs hit me, Bloom saved the day, swinging her bionic arm out wide, nailing both SPUDs with a roundhouse punch that Bruce Lee would've been proud of.

The harsh sounds of metal clanging against metal hurt my earballs as the SPUDs came crashing to the floor.

Bloom stood over me with eyes narrowed. She was breathing heavily, but she was okay.

Lexi was still in the corner, untouched.

And me? I was on the floor, trying to convince myself that it was all a bad dream. I rolled to my back and looked above my head. There was only one SPUD left, and he was carrying a folded up sheet of paper in his tiny stupid hand.

I felt for the letter in my back pocket, but it was gone.

"That thing's got my letter!" I shouted.

The metallic pitter patter of footsteps echoed down the aisle as the SPUD sped away from us.

"Oh no, you don't!" Bloom said, diving for the SPUD.

The SPUD tucked and rolled before Bloom could get to him. She landed on the ground, crying out in pain.

Popping back to his feet, the SPUD kept sprinting.

I pushed myself up and ran after the little machine, but it didn't matter how fast I was, the SPUD was faster. Plus, since he was a robot, he was able to do things that I couldn't in order to dodge my grabs, things I'd never seen a SPUD do before.

The SPUD leapt into the air, and used one of his hands to grab the front of the metal lockers, vaulting himself up to the hanging pipes along the ceiling.

"Get back here, ya little spider monkey!" I cried.

I ran down each aisle, keeping the SPUD in view the entire time. He moved like he didn't have an escape plan – like

114

he had no idea how to get out of the girl's locker room. He swung back and forth between the pipes along the ceiling until finally slipping off.

I thought for sure the SPUD was gonna break apart when he landed, but at the last second, he flipped and caught himself on both feet.

"Give it back!" I shouted, diving across the floor like I was stealing second base.

The SPUD hopped over me, and ran off in the opposite direction.

Bloom was waiting. She set both feet down and put her hands in front of her, ready to tackle the robot that had gone berserk.

The SPUD bounced back and forth as he ran toward her.

Bloom bounced back and forth to keep the SPUD in front of her.

Then the SPUD bounced left, and then immediately shot right.

Bloom went the wrong way, trying to catch him on the left, but instead got a mouthful of locker. She was *not* going to be a happy camper after that.

The SPUD faked her out, but he was still trying to find an exit.

Running to catch up with the SPUD, I saw him just before he turned back down the aisle with locker G42.

Lexi screamed, flailing her arms in the air, and ran out of the aisle so fast I thought she was gonna catch fire.

"Perfect," I said. "He's cornered! Come on!"

Bloom rubbed her mouth and joined me as we sprinted back to the very spot where the whole situation had started.

The SPUD was finished. He was standing perfectly still, staring at the brick wall that stopped his escape. Bloom and I were blocking his only way out.

"How the tables have turned," I said, trying to sound cool.

"Nerd," Bloom whispered.

The letter was in the SPUD's hands. Slowly the robot turned to face us, but not in a *creepy villain* kind of way – more like a *remote-controlled car switching directions* kind of way. The number on the SPUDs chest was "07." I'd have to remember to report that specific SPUD to the principal for stealing my stuff.

"Give it back to me," I ordered the SPUD.

The SPUD's eyes still glowed red like fire. He cocked his head like a confused dog. "*Negative. Order defies objective.*"

No idea what *that* meant.

"If you don't *give* it back, then I'll have to *take* it back!" I said, walking toward the trapped SPUD.

"*Negative*," the SPUD said again.

I braced myself, preparing to catch the SPUD if he decided to run again. And then, with one final leap, I dove after the SPUD that had my letter.

I managed to barely scrape the edge of the paper. It wasn't much, but it was enough to get it free from the SPUD's fingers.

At the same time, the SPUD flashed bright white, and I fell right *through* him, slamming my face against the brick wall at the end of the aisle.

The air was filled with smoke as I looked everywhere for the SPUD. "Where'd he go?"

"I don't know!" Bloom said, freaked. "I can't see anything!"

"*Where is he?*" I said, blinded by the smoke, sliding my hands on the floor looking for him. "He just disappeared? What the *junk?*"

When the smoke finally lifted, there was a scorched mark where the SPUD had been standing. My great-great-grandad's letter was on the floor. It was safe.

"He never ran past me," Bloom said. "I was watching like a hawk!"

Lexi was at the end of the aisle. "She's right. He didn't get out this way. We would've seen him!"

And just like that, the SPUD was gone.

24

The girl's locker room. 12:15 PM.

Lexi, Bloom, and I stared at the scorched spot where we had last seen the SPUD. I took the letter off the floor and tucked it away neatly in my back pocket.

Using my shoe, I pushed a path through the black burnt part of the concrete.

"Did that thing just self-destruct?" Bloom said.

"I think so," I said. "I didn't even know SPUDs had that option."

At that moment, a sickening scraping sound came from behind us. It was like a fork on the rough side of my mom's good dishes.

The three of us spun around, ready for another round with the SPUDs, but thankfully, it didn't come to that.

The sound came from Beck's little spider legs on the bottom of his helmet. My best friend crawled out of the vent that was under locker G42, dragging a dust-covered metal lunchbox behind him.

The two lights in his helmet switched off and he blinked a few times, letting his eyes adjust to the brighter part of the locker room. He crawled forward, toward the end of the aisle slowly, like he was hesitating.

"Hello?" he said aloud.

"Behind you," I sighed.

Beck turned around. "Oh!" he said with a smile. "Cool. I thought you guys bailed on me."

And then his eyes grew wide as he looked at the robotic limbs of SPUDs sprawled across the floor.

"Ummm…" he hummed. "What *happened* out here?"

"The robot rebellion," Bloom said. "It's the beginning of the end."

I knew she was joking, but it was a joke that hit a little too close to home.

"Some SPUDs attacked us," I said.

"Attacked?" Beck repeated. "No way. There's no way that happened!"

"It happened," Lexi whispered.

"Right after you walked into the vent," I explained. "A group of SPUDs cornered us here. They *attacked* us."

"Spuds aren't allowed to touch anyone," Beck said, concerned.

"Tell that to the SPUDs throwin' ninja kicks," Bloom said, inspecting her bionic arm. She pointed at a spot on the forearm. "Look. The metal's scraped up because of them."

"*Whaaaaaat?*" Beck said in disbelief. "Why'd they do that? Who ordered them to do it?"

"I'unno," I said, keeping an eye on the SPUD pieces, making sure none of them moved. "This shouldn't have been possible. Have they become self-aware? Is that what everybody is afraid of?"

"Like, the machines have developed their own brains, and have waged war against humanity?" Beck said.

"No," Bloom said. "I don't think so, because they acted like they were following orders. That one SPUD told Max that his order defied their objective. That means he was following *someone's* orders."

"It tried to take my letter." I threw my hands up and let them fall back to the floor. "It was here for the letter!"

"What?" Beck said. "No! Did it get it? Do you still have it?"

"I barely got it out of his hands," I said. "The SPUD blew itself up right afterward. It just… *popped*."

"So you still got it," Beck paused. "Good."

My squid friend stared at the scorched spot on the floor, studying it for a moment. And then, to my surprise, he *didn't* flip out about it.

"Bummer about the attack," he said.

"That's *all* you have to say?" I said. "Bummer?"

"What else do you want? You guys are fine, the letter's in your back pocket, and the school has one less SPUD."

I wasn't sure what to think. A SPUD attacking a human was a *big deal*, but Beck didn't even care.

"At least we still have your letter, but more importantly, we have this," Beck said, tapping the dusty lunchbox. "I found what we were looking for."

Bloom folded her arms and whispered. "Took ya long enough."

"It was pretty far in vent," Beck explained. "A hundred years of getting pulled slowly by air conditioning will move you move a good ten or twenty feet."

Beck's little spider legs climbed up his Tenderfoot Shell until he was above the open slot on the neck. Then he lowered himself down while tucking the spider legs into the suit. After a couple of buzzes and clicks, he had control of his robotic shell again.

Reaching down, Beck picked up the metal lunchbox and held it out to me. "Here," he said. "I didn't look in it yet... I wanted *you* to be the first one to open it."

I stared at the lunchbox. It was covered in dust, but still in great condition. The front of it had a picture of a blond haired kid holding a glowing sword above his head. A woman wearing a white robe stood next to him, and behind him was the giant head of a robot samurai mask or something. Stars were sprinkled all around the sides and back of the lunchbox.

As rocked as I was by the attack of the killer SPUDs, I was still thrilled at what prize the lunchbox had inside it. I just hoped it wasn't a hundred-year-old ham sammie.

I clicked the latch on the front of the lunchbox, making Lexi jump. She covered her mouth as she giggled and apologized.

"Here goes everything," I said, flipping open the lunchbox.

The inside was as clean as the day my great-great-grandad first shut it. The only two things in the box were a black mask and a monocle that had the Tenderfoot Industries logo on it.

Beck swirled his tentacles around underneath him.

I held the mask up to see it better. The cloth was the blackest black I had ever seen, and there was only one hole for the eyes.

"Is that… a ninja mask?" Bloom asked quietly as if she lost her voice.

I nodded. "Yeah, I think it is."

The four of us looked at each other, confused and excited at the same time.

"Guys…" I said softly. "What the *heck* is going on?"

25

The cafeteria. 12:25 PM.

My friends and I left the girl's locker room the same way we entered it – through the door behind the stage in the cafeteria. We wasted no time because none of us wanted another go at the freak SPUDs that had attacked us.

Bloom peeked her head out from behind the oversized velvet curtain on the stage that was so old it smelled like a wet dog. It was a smell that wafted over the entire lunchroom and on the hottest, sweatiest days, the stank was almost unbearable.

Once the coast was clear, Bloom peeled the curtain back and let Lexi, Beck, and me through.

The cafeteria was only half-full. There were still ten minutes left until lunch was over, so most of the students had moved into the lobby to hang out until the bell rung, and then even after that, we had fifteen minutes until our next class started.

I set the lunchbox on the table. The four of us watched it carefully like it was gonna sprout legs and run away.

"So," Bloom said, breaking the awkward silence. "How 'bout those SPUDs, huh? Those things are gonna fill my nightmares now."

"I know, right?" I said. "Were they reprogrammed or something?"

"Their eyes turned red," Lexi whispered. "SPUDs don't have red eyes."

"What if they've finally turned against humanity?" I said.

"You nerd," Bloom said. "You gotta stop watching all those classic *robots-take-over-the-world* movies."

"But it's totally possible!" I said.

"Get your head outta the clouds," Bloom said. "The obvious answer is usually the correct answer."

"What's the obvious answer?" Beck asked.

"Still workin' on that," Bloom said.

I slid my great-great-grandad's lunchbox across the table until it was in the middle of everyone. "Let's talk about this thing," I said, changing the subject. The idea of SPUDs freaking out on humanity was making me sweaty.

Beck flicked the cover off the top with one of his robot fingers.

The only things inside the box was a monocle with the Tenderfoot Industries logo on it, and a mask that looked like it had come from a ninja.

I pinched the black cloth and raised it up carefully like my arms were a crane.

"So what?" Lexi said. "Was he a ninja or something?"

"*No*," Bloom said immediately. "Ninjas weren't around a *hundred* years ago. They went extinct around *two* hundred years ago."

"That doesn't mean anything," I said. "What if the new ninjas were so good that nobody even knew they existed. What if they just got *really* good at what they did?"

Bloom sighed. "It's possible, but again, the most obvious answer is prob'ly the correct one."

I was confused. "The most obvious answer about what? About what happened to ninjas?"

"No," Bloom said, tapping the black mask. "The most obvious answer to why your relative had this mask."

"Why?"

"Simple. He was a criminal, and this was his bank-robbin' mask."

Everyone at the table laughed.

"Right," I said. "My eleven-year-old great-great-grandfather used to rob banks wearing *this* mask."

"It's either that or he actually *was* a ninja!" Bloom said.

"Put it on," Lexi said, smiling.

"Gross, no!" I said.

"Doooooo it," Bloom said, wearing a smile of her own.

"Yeah, man," Beck said. "Put on the hundred-year-old mask that's probably infected with diseases that have been cured."

"Ew," I said, leaning away from the mask even though I was still holding it in my fingers. "What if this thing has the chicken pox? Or like… some *polio*."

"Pretty sure polio was completely wiped out before that mask was even made," Bloom said. "Geez, you guys, don't you read books?"

Beck and I shook our heads at the same time.

"No."

"Nuh-uh."

Bloom rolled her eyes and slumped her shoulders. "So much for a brave adventurer. You can't even muster up enough courage to put on a *hat*."

To be fair, it wasn't *just* a hat. It was a crusty piece of fabric that had been sweating in a vent for the last hundred years. Who knew what kind of germs were living on that thing! According to science, the mask could've come to life itself by then!

"Come on," Lexi said. "Just see if it fits."

"No!" I said, but her puppy dog eyes were breaking down the wall I was trying to build. I grunted, wrinkling my nose. "Fiiiiiiine."

"Sucker," Beck laughed.

Carefully, I took the black mask and opened the bottom of it. Some gross dust fell from the inside. And then, with my face scrunched and my breath held, I pulled the mask over my head.

Once it was over my hair, I freaked and yanked it the rest of the way over my face.

I just wanted to be done with it.

But the bottom half of the mask ripped off and dropped around my neck like a scarf. The rest of the mask covered everything above my nose. I looked like such a dork.

"Happy?" I asked.

"*Very*," Lexi said.

I took the mask off my face along with the piece of fabric that was around my neck. "This thing *stinks*," I said. "*So* bad."

"A hundred years'll do that to ya," Beck said.

Rolling the fabric into a ball, I spun around in my chair and shot it like a basketball into a nearby garbage can.

"Dude!" Bloom said. "You can't just throw that away! It's part your family history!"

"It's just a stinky mask," I said. I was disappointed, but I couldn't tell exactly why.

My life had felt like I was living the same exact day every day since the start of the school year. Now, suddenly, there was a day different than any I've ever lived.

And it was beginning to scare me.

"This whole thing is turning out to be much stranger than I thought it'd be," I said. "I'm starting to have second thoughts about it all."

"No!" Beck said. "We're so close!"

"To what?" I asked. "So close to what? What's the endgame here? What's the purpose of all these clues?"

"That's kinda the answer we're searching for!" Beck said.

I shook my head, looking at the monocle in the shoebox. "Look, I'm still freaked about those SPUDs. After seeing what Patrick did with Mochi, and then getting attacked by the..."

Trailing off, I stared at the library doors through the tinted cafeteria windows.

My friends knew exactly what I was thinking.

"No way," Bloom said.

"It's the only explanation," I said. "The most obvious answer."

"You think Patrick reprogrammed those SPUDs?" Beck said.

My face felt hot. "He made his own SPUD out of the spare parts of other SPUDs, like some kind of *Frankenstein* SPUD. If *anyone* in the school is capable of taking control of them, it'd be Patrick!"

"He said Mochi wasn't connected to the mainframe," Beck said. "Mochi operates *outside* the system. The SPUDs that came after you guys couldn't have been on the system either because they'd just reset if anything was wrong with them!"

"It's Patrick," I said with confidence. "He's the one behind it all. He's *gotta* be!"

"Those SPUDs got to you *after* we talked to him," Beck said.

126

"Man," I said. "It's always the quiet geniuses that turn out to be evil villains, right?"

"Whoa," Bloom said, annoyed. "Drop anchor, dude. We're talkin' about an eleven-year-old boy – not the next supervillain bent on world domination. It's *Patrick*. He's *harmless*."

"That's what he *wants* us to think," I said, frustrated. "But I'm *done* thinking. There's only one way to find out whether he's behind this or not."

I grabbed the monocle, stuffed it into the front pocket of my jeans, and marched for the front doors of the cafeteria.

"*Where* are you going?" Lexi said.

"To find Patrick!"

26

Back in the library. 12:35 PM.

We had to filter our way through the crowd of students in the lobby in order to get to the library. Most of the kids had finished lunch and were waiting for the bell to ring.

They were laughing, and joking, and flirting with each other. Nobody had any idea that Buchanan School was home to an evil villain secretly working in the library, building his... evil villain... *machines*, and stuff – *death rays* and *laser sharks* or something.

Microscopic laser sharks! Oh man, could you imagine? Holy wow!

I was so focused on my mission that I didn't even hold the door open for my friends – didn't even *wait* for them when I got into the library.

But when I got to the room Patrick used, he wasn't there. Mochi wasn't either.

"Are you nuts?" Bloom said when she caught up with me.

Lexi was with her, but didn't say anything.

"Any kid that can take control of and reprogram SPUDs should be stopped," I said. "He's dangerous."

"First of all," Bloom said. "You have no proof that he did anything. You're just assuming he did."

"The most obvious answer, right?" I said, repeating Bloom's own words.

"That's just it," Bloom said. "It's not the most obvious answer to me!"

When Beck caught up to us, I ignored everything Bloom was saying.

"He's not here," I said to Beck.

Beck scanned the room with his eyes. "There's gotta be proof somewhere in here, right? There can't be *this* much junk just laying around without *something* that shows he messed with those SPUDs."

"Let's start looking," I said, stepping onto the single path in the room. "I'll start at his desk. You look everywhere else."

"You guys can't just do this!" Bloom said. "None of this stuff is yours!"

I ignored her again.

The table where Patrick worked was filthy, cluttered with stacks of paper with scribbled notes. He filled each sheet until there wasn't *any* space left to write anything at all. And this went on for what looked like *thousands* of pages.

Beck was pushing stuff around to make a new path to walk through. Robot parts tumbled off the stacks of papers and boxes, falling against other stacks of even more boxes.

"Careful," I said. "You don't want to hurt any evidence."

"If there *is* any evidence," Bloom said from the door, her arms folded.

"There's gotta be *something*," I said. "Even if it's something that has to do with Mochi, it'll be enough to take to Principal Green."

"What's a Mochi?" Lexi asked from the door.

"Mochi is a SPUD he created," I explained. "Patrick used parts from other SPUDs to make his own that's *not* connected to the mainframe."

Lexi paused. "Sweet," she said.

"*Not* sweet," I said. "That's the reason why I know he's behind those SPUD attacks."

Lexi made a face as she watched Beck and me tear through all of Patrick's stuff. I wasn't sure if she was upset or not, but being me, I kept searching with a determined look on my face. For a second, I wondered if I was actually worried about Patrick, or if Lexi thought I looked cool.

"Look," Beck said.

I glanced over my shoulder at my best friend. He was holding what looked like the hands from a SPUD.

"We got 'im," I said.

Lifting my knees, I waded through the sea of papers until I reached Beck. He was standing over an open box that had other parts of SPUDs on it. The front of the box was stamped "*DECOMMISSIONED*," in red. "*For Patrick*" was written with black marker.

"What's 'decommissioned'?" I asked.

"It means those SPUD parts weren't being used for anything anymore," Bloom said. "The way he got that box was legit though. It's even got Patrick's name on it. You noobs. The school *gave* him those parts!"

I shook my head, taking the SPUD hand from Beck and shaking it at Bloom. "Doesn't mean he didn't use these for his own evil *take-over-the-world* plans."

"Do you hear yourself?" Bloom said way too loudly. Like, I'm pretty sure the whole library heard her shout at me. "You're full-throttle crazy right now!"

A voice erupted from behind Bloom and Lexi. "*What?*"

"Uh-oh," Bloom said as she stepped aside. "Busted. Again."

Patrick stood at the door to his workspace, staring at the damage Beck and I had done. Both his hands were on his head as his chest heaved up and down. His own personal SPUD, Mochi, was standing right next to him.

"*What're you guys doing to my stuff?*" Patrick said angrily.

I was going to call Patrick out, but couldn't because right at that moment, a group of SPUDs appeared behind him, all with the same fire-red eyes as the ones back in the locker room.

Of course he was traveling with his own army of SPUD bodyguards. What villain *wouldn't* do that if they had them?

Dropping the SPUD part in my hand, I found what little voice remained in my throat. "Whoopsies."

27

So there I was trapped in a room guarded by a dozen tiny robots that were reprogrammed to be bad guys, and all I could think about was my underwear.

Thanks, Mom, for making me so freaked out about clean underwear that it was the only thing on my mind in *any* dangerous situation!

Patrick was still at the door with the dozen or so SPUDs behind him. I *knew* he had built himself an army. I *knew* I was right about him being some kind of supergenius villain. And I *knew* I'd totally be a hero when I uncovered his secret!

I *knew* it. Until…

Patrick turned around when he felt one of the SPUDs bump his leg. His face went from shock to horror when he saw how many there were.

He stumbled back into the room with Bloom and Lexi doing their best to catch him before he fell.

They didn't, and he crashed into a short pile of books.

Mochi strolled into the room with a little too much *pop* in his step. I'm not sure he knew what was happening.

"What's going on?" Patrick said with a hint of panic in his voice. "What're these SPUDs doing here? They're here to take Mochi away, aren't they?"

Mochi plopped himself down on an uneven stack of boxes, sitting crisscrossed and bobbing back and forth to music that nobody else could hear.

"Wait," I said. "So you're *not* the one behind the evil SPUDs?"

"What're you talking about? No!" Patrick boomed. "I'd *never* do something like that! Do you know how stupid that'd be? I'd get busted for messing with school property!"

"Huh," I grunted, not knowing what to say because I was embarrassed.

Bloom just shook her head at me with a smug smile on her face.

Her smile disappeared when the small army of SPUDs flooded the door.

The Spud at the front of the group was the same one from the locker room – the one with the "07" on his chest – the one that *exploded* in front of us. He even had scorch marks all over his body.

Bloom saw it too. She touched my arm and pointed at the robot.

"It must've been a trick," I said. "The smoke distracted us while he got away, like some kind of vanishing act."

Bloom nodded.

I knew I had to do something. The SPUDs from the locker room didn't hesitate to attack us, and these probably wouldn't either. And being trapped in a tiny room filled with junk was the worst possible place for something bad to happen.

All I needed to do was get the SPUDs away from my friends, so I tapped Beck on the shoulder. When he looked at me, he nodded, knowing that I wanted him to follow my lead.

At once, I broke out, sprinting toward the only door to the room with Beck doing the same.

Mochi laughed, thinking it was a game, and ran with us.

"Mochi, stop!" Patrick shouted, but his little robot friend didn't listen.

Pushing the ball of my foot into the carpet, I leapt over the SPUDs in a single bounce, sailing clear over their little robot heads as they all craned their necks to watch me.

I heard the door to Patrick's office slam shut behind me. Beck must've grabbed the door after he jumped out to keep the others safe.

As soon as I hit the floor on the other side, I rolled across the carpet and bounced back to my feet. Beck landed perfectly right next to me. Surprisingly, so did Mochi.

"Nice," I said to Patrick's robot friend.

"Mo-chi! Mo-chi! Mo-chi!" the little robot chanted pumping his fists in the air.

"Split up!" I said as I took off in one direction.

Beck took off in another direction, and Mochi in yet another, still pumping his fists in the air and chanting his own name.

Going in three different directions should've split the SPUDs into three groups, but the plan backfired.

All the SPUDs came after *just* me.

"*Whaaaaaat?*" I said, running down different aisles of books in the library.

You'd think that a dozen robots chasing after a kid would be one of the noisiest action sequences ever, but it was just the opposite. It was the quietest chase that ever happened in the entire history of the world ever.

The soft sound of my sneakers hitting the carpet was the only thing that made any kind of noise. The SPUDs chasing after me made almost no sound at all. They were amazingly graceful for being klutzy robots.

I turned the corner at the staircase in the middle of the library, hoping the librarian would see me, but she wasn't even there. She must've been at lunch or something. In fact, the entire library was empty.

"Wonderful," I huffed as I ran up the steps, skipping every other one until I was on the second floor.

The SPUDs crouched on all fours, jumping like monkeys onto the handrail of the staircase, and then up to the second floor.

Beck was down below, following as the SPUDs chased after me. Mochi was running in circles, still pumping his weird little robo-fists.

I was beginning to think Mochi wasn't the sharpest knife in the drawer.

From the second floor, I had a clear view of the room that Patrick, Lexi, and Bloom were stuck in. Patrick was struggling with the door like it was locked.

"What do I do?" I shouted to Beck.

"Throw me the letter!" he said.

"Throw you the letter?"

"That's what they're after! Throw it down so they don't get it!"

I tried feeling for the letter in my back pocket, but before I could do anything, I felt the tiny hands of several SPUDs clutch at my clothing.

The dozen robots that were chasing me finally caught up, swarming my entire body. I panicked, spinning around and head-banging to get them off me.

One of the SPUDs fell to the floor, catching the underside of my foot, and I slipped backwards.

I stumbled, trying to get my balance back, but it was too late.

My side hit the railing, and my body flipped over the edge. The SPUDs that were on me gracefully hopped to safety on the railing, like they had finished their job. They become lifeless statues looking over the library.

And there I was, clutching the metal bars on the railing so I wouldn't fall. The floor wasn't far below me, but I'm kind of afraid of heights so it *felt* far.

I know, right? A daredevil afraid of heights. Pfft.

"Dude," I said to Beck. "Catch me!"

"Are you nuts?" Beck said.

"Your arms are robotic! You can catch a meteorite!"

"Throw me the letter first!"

"*What?*"

"The letter from your ancestor! Toss it down so it's safe! Then I'll catch you!"

I heard a series of beeps come from below me, but I had no idea what it was.

And then the SPUDs on the second floor came to life again. They were gathering around the spot where I was hanging.

I wasn't thinking straight. If I threw Beck the letter, then he might see that there weren't any other codes on it, but if I kept it from him, the SPUDs would get their metal paws on it.

"Fine!" I said, letting go of the railing with one hand. I took the letter from my back pocket and tossed it down to Beck who caught it like a pro.

A door slammed open across the room, crashing against the wall, and then I heard Bloom's voice.

"It's Beck!" she shouted. "Beck's the one controlling the SPUDs! We saw him do it just a second ago! He pushed some buttons on his arm, and they all started moving toward you!"

"What?" I said, confused and still hanging from the railing on the second floor. I turned my body and looked over my shoulder to see what was going on.

Beck clutched my letter as he spun around. And then he bent down, grabbed something, and stood back up, holding it out in front of him.

Lexi slid to a stop several feet away from Beck. Patrick did the same right behind her, his face as pale as a ghost.

Bloom was still back at the door. She was picking herself off the ground and wiping something wet off the side of her jeans. "So gross!" she shouted.

"Don't even *think* about taking another step!" Beck growled at Patrick.

I couldn't believe what I was watching. Everything had happened so fast that my brain felt like it was mushy cereal that was about to get poured down the drain.

Patrick stepped forward. I think he had tears in his eyes. "*Please...* don't hurt him!" his voice cracked.

There, hanging in the air by Beck's death grip, was Mochi.

28

Still in the library. 12:55 PM.

I was still hanging from the railing with one hand, looking down at the crazy scene below me.

My best friend had my great-great-grandad's letter and was holding Mochi prisoner with both his hands.

Bloom was furious, but stood her ground. The side of her jeans were soaked in something, but I didn't know what.

Patrick was on his knees, begging for Beck to release Mochi.

Lexi was behind all of them, covering her mouth with her hands.

"Beck, what're you doing?" I asked, confused. I couldn't believe my best friend was doing what he was doing. He *had* to have a good reason for it!

Beck's Tenderfoot Shell didn't move, but he swirled around in his glass helmet, staring daggers at me.

"This life," he growled. "This life is *so* boring. *You're* so boring! You're nothing but a poser! A wannabe action-junkie who's too afraid of change!"

I wasn't sure what to say. "Um… okaaaay…"

"Finally, something exciting turned up!" Beck continued. "Something you're not even worthy of! So guess what, Max? *I'm* taking it from you! I'm taking this *adventure* and keeping it for myself!"

"Come on, man!" I called down from the railing. "It doesn't need to be like this! Just put Mochi down!"

Y'know, hanging from a ledge will really clear a guy's head. I realized what was important. I didn't care about whether Beck knew the truth about the letter. All I cared about was Mochi not getting hurt.

"Dude, keep the letter!" I said. "It's yours, alright?"

Beck's eyes narrowed as if he wasn't sure he should trust me.

"I don't want that dumb thing anyway!" I said. "You're right! I'm a poser! I'm nothing but a daredevil wannabe! I'm not even worthy of my great-great-grandad's legacy, alright? I'm a poser! I'm a failure!"

It bummed me out to say it because I really *felt* it. I *was* a failure.

"Why should I believe you?" Beck said.

"Why *shouldn't* you?" I said. "Look at me! I'm hanging by a thread here! I give up! Just take it and let Mochi go! You'll walk away, we'll walk away, and no one will get hurt!"

I thought I was getting somewhere with Beck and that he was actually considering letting Mochi go, but Patrick killed that vibe.

Patrick hobbled forward, clutching both hands in front of him. "*Please* let him go!" he said weakly. "He might just be a *robot* to you, but he's my *only* friend! He's like my brother!"

I felt for Patrick – I really did. Beck was like *my* brother, but I was pretty sure our friendship was kaput. It's not like I'd come to school the next day and be all, "S'up, man? Rough day yesterday, huh? Welp, let's be besties!"

Beck swirled in his helmet again. He was losing what little cool he had left. "Stay back!" he shouted at Patrick.

Up until then, Mochi had been calm in Beck's hand. His eyes were moving back and forth like he was watching what was going on, but then it was like everything clicked, and he started flipping out.

Mochi's arms and legs moved wildly, struggling to free himself from Beck's grip.

"Daddy, help!" Mochi shouted.

"Whoa, he called him daddy?" Bloom said loudly enough that I could hear her.

"That's kinda messed up," Lexi said.

"You're scaring him!" Patrick said. "Please let him go already!"

"You programmed a robot to be *afraid?*" I said from the railing. "Who programs a robot with *fear?*"

Beck continued to struggle with Mochi. Patrick's little creation was writhing around now, screaming for help. His little arms waved back and forth so fast that they were a blur that made contact with Beck's glass helmet. Every clink that came from the glass made Beck flinch.

And then Beck held Mochi out in front of him with one hand. He placed his other hand at the base of Mochi's neck and stuck his finger into a small slot under the robot's head.

It was an opening that every SPUD had behind the bottom of their head – it was the "off" switch.

Mochi's body jerked, and then he went limp. The screen on his face blipped, turning black.

"*Noooooo!*" Patrick screamed, tripping over himself as he jolted forward.

Beck said nothing.

Digging his fingers into the floor, Patrick practically flew to his feet in an all out sprint at Beck.

But Beck didn't move his body. Instead, the glass helmet he was inside of lifted up off the Tenderfoot Shell, and his mechanical spider legs crept out, grabbing both Mochi and the letter.

Everything that happened next was a blur.

A flash of light burst from Beck's helmet just as Patrick tackled the Tenderfoot Shell. They both rolled across the floor.

On the railing above me were the same flashes of light along with the stink of burnt rubber.

And then everything was quiet again.

Beck's Tenderfoot Shell was on the floor next to Patrick, but Beck's helmet, the letter, and Mochi were all gone.

The SPUDs were gone too.

All that remained were the scorched spots where they *used* to be.

29

The library. 1:05 PM.

Lexi was freaking out, clutching at her hair with both her hands. "Where'd Beck go? His *head* blew up! And the little robots! They all self-destructed! *What's happening?*"

"Little help here?" I said, still hanging from the railing.

Bloom ran over, and even though she had every intention of catching me, she was still just an eleven-year-old girl. I should've known better, but my arm was killing me.

She held out both arms and stood under me. "I gotcha!"

…

I helped her to her feet after landing right on top of her. I felt horrible.

"…my organs," she said as she let me help her off the ground.

"Which ones?"

She paused. "*All* of them."

"I'm *so* sorry!"

"It's cool," she said. "Wouldn't be the worst thing that happened to me today. You didn't see me slip back there, did you?"

I pointed at the side of her jeans. They were wet from her thigh down to the middle of her shin. "Is that what happened to your pants?"

"Yeah," she said. "I slipped on Patrick's weird fruit basket."

"Beck's controlling the SPUDs," I said to Bloom.

"Obvi," she said. "But how? How is that even possible?"

"He's good at computer things," I said, and then about slapped myself in the face. "We were in the SPUD control center earlier!"

"You were?" Lexi said.

I nodded. "We were going to the dungeon. The SPUD mainframe was on the way, and he was doing something by himself in there. I should've seen it earlier."

Lexi put her hand on my back. "There was no way you would've known."

Patrick was still on the floor, staring at the ceiling. The headless Tenderfoot Shell was next to him. His voice was weak, and his lip was quivering. He was on the verge of a complete breakdown. "They teleported…" he said. "Beck used my tele-pin… that flash of light and smell of burnt rubber is always what's left after the tele-pin is used. He must've *stolen* my tele-pins."

"They teleported?" Bloom said.

"You said that thing couldn't teleport anything bigger than a basketball!" I said.

"Beck and his helmet *aren't* bigger than a basketball," Patrick said. "And since he was only holding Mochi, they teleported just fine."

I looked at the Tenderfoot Shell on the floor. "That's why it was *just* the head."

And there was no chance of finding Beck by using his Holo Pen. The pen was in the robotic suit's hand.

Patrick sat up and put his arms on his knees. His head drooped into the open spot over his chest. His shaky, muffled voice spoke. "Mochi can't be switched off for more than fifteen minutes or else his whole system will reboot. If that happens, he'll go back to being a normal SPUD. His memory will be wiped. The robot will be a SPUD, but Mochi will *die*."

"What?" Bloom asked, sitting crisscrossed on the floor next to Patrick.

Patrick continued. "Mochi isn't connected to the SPUD mainframe. That's why he has his own personality. But his own system isn't strong enough to keep that wall in place unless he's powered on at all times. If he's off for too long, his system will reboot and wipe his brain clean."

I was only half-listening, still trying to wrap my head around the fact that my best friend just turned into a bad guy that *teleported* to escape. "But Beck!" I said. "Where did Beck go? Where'd he and his little SPUD army go?"

"I don't know!" Patrick said, still keeping his head buried. And then I realized *why* he was hiding his face. It's because he was crying.

Bloom, Lexi, and I looked at each other. I shrugged my shoulders because I didn't know what to do.

"I never know where any of that stuff reappears," Patrick said. "Still workin' on figuring that out." He paused, and then fought to get the rest of his words out. "*Mochi* was helping me with the equations!"

Lexi sat down on the other side of Patrick, rubbing his back as he sobbed. Bloom was still staring at me, unsure of what to say. Crying kids made her uneasy.

I pulled a chair out from one of the tables and took a seat. My eyes were dry, but I could've broken down just as easily as Patrick had.

Defeated. That's the word I'd use to describe how I felt. And not just, like, I *lost*, but I was *completely, totally,* and *stupidly* defeated.

We *all* were.

I felt like I had hit rock bottom, and not from the hard landing on top of Bloom, who, BTW, was alright.

My great-great-grandad's letter was gone, but that wasn't even the worst part. No, the worst part was that my bestest friend in the whole world *wasn't* my bestest friend anymore.

I had never felt more alone in my life.

And then, I covered my face with my hands… and I cried.

30

The library. Like, a minute later.

I managed to keep my face hidden from my friends. I wiped away any evidence of tears before they even left my eyes.

After a minute, Patrick switched from sobbing to holding his knees while rocking back and forth. He just kept repeating, "He *took* him... he *took* him... he *took* him..."

Bloom came over and sat in the chair next to me. I knew she knew I was crying. That's not exactly the easiest thing to hide. The side of her jeans were still wet with whatever she slipped in back in Patrick's room.

"You okay?" she asked softly, putting her robotic hand on mine. It's crazy how her robotic hand *didn't* feel like a robotic hand. It wasn't cold like you'd expect, and she was so gentle with it.

"No," I answered honestly.

Patrick picked himself off the ground and lumbered toward us. He sniffled and then pushed his hand under his nose. Reaching into his pocket, he pulled out the black cassette that Beck and I had given him earlier – the one that had "*NOT NINJA SECRETS*" written on it.

"You can have this back," he said, dropping the cassette on the table.

I didn't say anything because whatever was on the cassette didn't even seem important anymore.

"I got the video off the cassette," he said, clearing his throat. "Sent it to your Holo Pen, but I didn't watch it. Y'know, 'cause of privacy and stuff."

After that, Patrick walked back to the scorched carpet where Beck had teleported with Mochi. He sat on the floor next to the spot and stared at it.

I took the Holo Pen from behind my ear and stood it on end.

Lexi got up from the floor and joined Bloom and me at the table.

And then I tapped the side of my Holo Pen, bringing up the "Messages" menu. It was a flat, blue screen that hovered above the pen.

There it was – Patrick's message to me that contained the video recorded at the beginning of the century.

Before I went any further, I looked at Bloom and then at Lexi.

I pushed my finger through the spot on the hologram that said I had a message.

The flat hologram flickered, and then switched to a blank screen.

It played for about five seconds before flickering again, and there, blinking at me, was my great-great-grandfather as a kid.

"He looks like you," Lexi said, awed.

She was right. Except for the crazy hair, he could've been my brother. It was weird seeing him at eleven years old staring back at me, but even weirder when he started talking.

"Hello, human flesh children of Buchanan School," he said with a smile. "My name is Chase Cooper, and I'm a sixth grade ninja. It's kind of a secret so, y'know, don't say anything about it…"

A girl's voice spoke in the video somewhere offscreen. She must've been the one recording him. "Chase! It's recording! You can't say that when the camera's rolling!"

"Zoe's filming a documentary about how leftover dog food is repackaged and sold to students during lunch," Chase continued. "The worst part? *Everyone* knows, but *nobody* cares."

Bloom scrunched her nose. "Ew. People ate dog food back then?"

The girl offcamera spoke again. "Chase…"

Chase ignored the girl's plea. "It's almost as if," he said, "students *want* to eat sloppy dog food for lunch! Everyone, that is, *except* Zoe."

"Oh, he was joking," Bloom said.

"*Chase*…" said the girl, who obviously must've been Zoe.

"I'm only *kidding!*" Chase paused, and then added, "Zoe actually likes the dog food lunches too."

"*Chase!*" Zoe shouted one last time, and then the video went blank.

Lexi, Bloom, and I looked back and forth at each other, confused.

"That was it?" Lexi asked, annoyed and disappointed. "*That's* the message he decided to send to his family a hundred years in the future?"

Bloom smirked. "I, for one, am not surprised. Max is a weirdo, and it only makes sense that the rest of his family are weirdos too."

I gotta admit, seeing a goofy message like that from someone in my family *did* make me feel a little more *normal*.

The hologram flickered, and then Chase's face stared back at me again.

"Uh, hey," Chase said, this time awkwardly. "So I guess I'm leaving you a message, whoever you are. I mean, I don't know what I'm thinking by recording this. There are a couple clues you'd have to solve in order to find it, but… if you *did* find it, then kudos to you."

"What's kudos mean?" Bloom asked. "Gratz?"

I nodded.

"And if you found this, then it means that you're, like, related to me or something, right?" Chase said.

"Right," I answered like he could hear me.

Lexi snickered.

"So I'll keep this short because I have a history of talking too much," Chase continued. "I just want to say that, whoever you are, you're awesome. Like, way more awesome than you think. If you're anything like me then you're probably super hard on yourself about dumb things, and if there was one message I wanted to send to you, it'd be to stop doing that."

I watched my great-great-grandfather on the hologram. The things he said were inspiring and hopeful, but he had no idea he was talking to a kid that had just crash-landed his own life.

"The whole time I've been a student at Buchanan," Chase said, "my life has gotten crazier and crazier every single week, and I know that it's gonna get even *crazier* after I'm done recording this. Sometimes I feel like a *failure*. Sometimes I even *fail*, but… I never stay down. I *always* get back up, and *always* keep going. Sixth grade is rough, but Cooper's are *rougher*. Is that a word?"

I nodded, again acting like he was really right in front of me.

"It's crazy to believe," Chase said. "But I *am* a ninja – just take my word for it. Am I a traditional ninja? No. I'm the *new* kind."

"*I knew it!*" Lexi said.

"Wow," Bloom said. "He actually *was* a ninja."

Chase took a breath in the video. "There's a lot more to Buchanan than anyone realizes, and I'm *sure* it's the same way for you, which is why I left my mask for you to find. I *hope* you found it by now. I promise it's clean."

"Biscuits," I said under my breath, remembering that I had tossed the mask in the garbage can back in the cafeteria.

Chase kept talking. "So that's it, dude. You're my family so you're cool. I've learned a lot this year – the *hard* way, and I wanted to pass it down to you because… I'd hate to leave a message that just said, "S'up, man? Welp, see ya later."

Lexi giggled.

"I hate sounding like an afterschool special," Chase said, "but sometimes that's the *only* way to sound – especially if I want to keep this message short. Shorter is prob'ly better, huh? That way you can figure it all out for yourself. I mean, this is my legacy I'm passing down, but you've got your own legacy to leave, amirite?"

I watched as Chase unfolded a sheet of paper that he had written on. The top of the paper said, "*Chase Cooper's 5 Rules for Being Cool.*"

"Kind of a dork, isn't he?" Bloom said.

"I think it's cute," Lexi said. "I guess *all* Coopers are charming."

Lexi blushed when she said it. I smiled. Bloom huffed.

Chase read his rules out loud. "One – always stand for the things you believe in. Two – always be cool to everyone, no matter who they are. Three – Always be yourself by being true to yourself. Four – Always work hard at being a better version of who you were yesterday. And five – Never lose hope."

Chase paused for a moment, blinking into the camera. "That last one's something I have a problem with – losing hope. Luckily, I got the best friends in the world. They remind me why I need to keep going, *especially* when I wanna quit."

I shook my head. Maybe I was wrong about my great-great-grandad. I didn't think we would've had anything in common, but it turned out that we had more in common than I thought.

"Also," Chase said. "If you ever get injured wearing the ninja mask, you can call it a *ninjury*." He laughed at his own joke while his eyebrows bounced up and down. "Get it? Like… an injury, but… yeah."

"You've got his sense of humor," Bloom sighed, looking at me. "How *terribly* sad."

Chase smiled in the video, and then he held up his hand, parting his fingers so they made a "V" shape. "Live long and prosper," he said at last.

The video went blank, and my brain felt like mush – like it had packed its bags and was headed to Florida because it just couldn't *even* anymore.

31

The library. Like, another minute later.

I tapped the side of my Holo Pen and switched off the display. I didn't know what to say so I kept my mouth shut.

"Huh," Lexi said. "So that was… *different*. It's not everyday you get a video message from someone in your family telling you they were a ninja. Especially an *eleven-year-old* ninja. He must've trained really hard."

Lexi was kidding, but I didn't feel like laughing. I felt terrible too, because after she made her joke, she got up from the table and joined Patrick on the floor. I'm sure she was just trying to help him feel better, but part of me thought it was because I was being a downer.

Bloom tapped the table in front of me with her robot hand. "You in there?"

I nodded, still staring at the Holo Pen as I spun it in circles in my fingers.

"Good," she said seriously. "Because you're running out of time."

"What?" I asked, annoyed and confused. "Running out of *what* time?"

"You need to pull yourself together," Bloom said.

Her face told me that she wasn't gonna let me off easy.

But everything in my body was done. I was nothing. I was *mush* sitting in a chair.

"What am *I* gonna do?" I asked.

Bloom shook her head and made a face like she was blown away. "Were you just here? Did you hear anything that message said to you?"

"The message from my great-great-grandad?"

"Uhhhh, was there *another* message that I could be talking about?"

"No."

"Then, yes. *That* message."

"That message was recorded a hundred years ago," I said, upset. "It's got nothing to do with today. It's got nothing to do with *right* now."

"Are you kidding me?" Bloom snapped, sitting up in her chair. "*That* message is the whole *reason* why today even happened."

I looked at Bloom, not sure what she meant.

"It's your great-great-grandfather's fault that *anything* today even happened," Bloom said. "He decided to send a letter into the future – a letter that had you running around the school chasing after clues."

She was right. My day would've been exactly the same as every other day if I hadn't been called to the principal's office that morning.

"So anything *bad* that happened is because of your great-great-grandpa," Bloom said. "But y'know what? That's obviously *not* what Chase would've wanted."

Bloom was right about that too.

"You have the choice to make everything turn out good right now," she said harshly, leaning forward so only I could hear her.

"Nothing good can possibly come from this," I said, not sure whether I felt excited or scared. "It's all bad. We lost. I lost."

Bloom pressed her lips together and stared me dead in the eye.

"You want me to get that letter back?" I said. "I don't even care about it. I'm glad it's gone!"

"You don't mean that."

"I do!" I said, surprising myself. "I'm no daredevil! I'm no hero! I *thought* I wanted adventure, but not like this. It cost me *too* much. I lost my best friend today because of it!"

Bloom sighed.

We sat in silence for a minute.

And then she spoke again, softly. "I feel bad that Beck burned you today. I know that your friendship is over because of what he did. You're right – you lost your best friend today, but you know who else lost their best friend?"

I looked at Patrick who was still on the floor. It ate away at me that Mochi was kidnapped by Beck, but I didn't know what to do. All I knew was that I was heartbroken and scared.

"I'm afraid, okay?" I said. "I already messed everything up, and I'm so afraid of messing up anything else that I can't even move!"

"Okay," Bloom said. "Then you can just sit here, *soaked* in fear. You can sit here until school is over. You can come back tomorrow, and everything will be *kinda* back to normal. Beck's gonna get busted. All we gotta do is tell Principal Green what he did. He might swim in detention for a week, maybe two, but he'll be back. You two won't be friends anymore, but he'll still be around."

I swallowed hard, feeling short of breath because I knew what she was getting at.

"But Patrick," Bloom said. "Patrick's *wrecked*. He lost his best friend today too, but Mochi's gone forever. At least, he will be in a few minutes."

My mind was racing. Pieces of Chase's message repeated in my head. Everything Bloom was saying. Flashes of Beck just before he disappeared with Mochi filled my brain.

"Or… you can do something about it," Bloom said, waving her hands in the air. "This adventure you were looking for? You *got* it. You *got* what you wanted."

I said nothing. I didn't need to. Bloom wasn't trying to get me to talk – she was trying to open my eyes.

I *did* want something more from life, and I got it when Principal Green gave me the letter from the capsule.

But the way it turned out wasn't as cool as I thought it'd be. It cost more than I thought it would.

It cost me my best friend, and even worse, Mochi, who was like Patrick's brother.

My gut wrenched. "But what can I do?"

"*Anything* you can," Bloom said. "What did Chase say? You *wanna* quit right now, but I *won't* let you. I *won't* let you be an unstuck sticker."

My eyes met Bloom's. She was determined. She was hardcore. And she was right, like she was most of the time anyway. I couldn't let myself be an unstuck sticker sitting at the bottom of a dark locker.

My heart pounded so hard that it felt like it was trying to escape from my ribcage. It was like everything black and white had become color to me, and I suddenly knew exactly what I had to do. The fact that I had very little time to think about it only made it easier for me.

I wasn't going to let my great-great-grandad down, but more importantly, I wasn't going to let Patrick down.

For a second, I thought about the villains in my comic books. Every single one of them had a point in their life when they decided to be the bad guy – it was their origin story. I didn't want today to be Patrick's origin story.

I inhaled deeply, slowly.

Bloom knew me so well that I didn't even have to say anything. She tapped me on the side of my arm with the butt of her fist. "*There* he is," she said.

I stood from the table, determined. "It's Mochi-savin'-time."

I never was good at one-liners.

32

The library. Like, even yet **another** *minute later.*

Patrick led us back to his workspace, panicked that it might've been too late to save Mochi. After all, it had been almost ten minutes since Beck disappeared with the little guy.

"I don't know," he said between his quick breaths as he searched through his office. "I don't know where Beck could've traveled to."

The stacks of boxes where I first saw the tele-pins were toppled over, and all the little buttons were missing.

"So he took everything?" I said. "Are there *any* tele-pins left? Maybe I could use one and teleport to the same place he did."

"No!" Patrick said. "That's insane. Like I said, it can only teleport small things the size of a basketball."

I groaned, frustrated. "And you have no idea where these things end up?"

Patrick stopped and shook his head. He was embarrassed. "That's something I'm still working on."

"So what happens to the tele-pin once you use it?" Lexi asked.

"It's gone," Patrick said. "Teleported away, but I made, like, a hundred of them. I was planning on finding them before I ran out."

"Well, Beck isn't dumb," Lexi said. "He wouldn't use it if he didn't know what he was doing."

"We first saw it happen with the SPUD in the locker room," Bloom said. "Number Seven! Remember? Creepy robot just vanished in front of our eyes."

"Which means Beck tested it," Patrick said, and then stopped searching the stacks of papers. "Look, here's the deal. If Beck's using this thing, then he *has* to know where he's ending up, right? He's not crazy enough to use it if he didn't, right?"

"Why's that such a big deal?" Lexi asked. "Why is it so important to know where things will teleport to?"

"Because if you don't, then you could end up inside a wall," Patrick said. "You could end up inside *anything* actually. What if you teleported six feet underground?"

"You wouldn't need a coffin then," Bloom joked.

"Exactly," Patrick said.

"Beck has to know that," I said. "But can he control where he ends up?"

"No," Patrick said. "That's my problem. I don't know where *any* of the stuff goes when it teleports. Could be in my backyard – could be on the moon."

TELEPORTING
+ ABOVE GROUND
= GOOD!

TELEPORTING
+ BELOW GROUND
= BAD!

"That's responsible," Bloom said, grinning.

"It's progress," Patrick said. "I've created something that scientists have been experimenting with for years, and I did it with a bunch of backyard junk."

156

"Then why is it still sitting in your dumpy room back here?" Lexi asked.

"Because I don't know where anything ends up!" Patrick was exasperated. "Have you been listening to any of what I've been saying?"

Bloom folded her arms. "Makes sense."

"Guys!" I said. "Can we focus? Mochi's running out of time!"

Patrick rubbed his face, thinking aloud. "Beck can't control where he's ending up, but he's not dumb enough to use the tele-pin if he didn't *know* where he'd end up. That means it's somewhere safe, but none of us can use it because we're too big."

"Wait," I said. "Can he teleport *back* after that?"

"No," Patrick said. "It's a one-way trip."

Bloom snapped her fingers because she knew what I was thinking.

"That means he's close!" I said. "Because the SPUD from the locker room was with the group that got to us in here! Wherever they are is close enough to get back to the school right away."

Patrick tapped at his forehead with all his fingers while squeezing his eyes shut. "Beck still wouldn't risk it if he were teleporting anywhere dangerous, and '*anywhere dangerous*' would be anywhere *inside* the school."

"Boo-yah-ha!" Lexi said.

"He's gotta be outside," I said.

"It's the safest place," Patrick said.

I took the lead, sprinting across the library as my friends tried to keep up.

If Mochi was anywhere near the school, I was gonna find him.

But I knew that Beck was gonna be right there next to him.

Patrick said the tele-pin was a one-way trip. Beck wasn't going to be able to disappear again, which meant I was running headfirst into trouble.

33

I slammed open the doors to the front of the school. Bloom and Patrick were right behind me. Lexi went straight to the front offices to tell Principal Green what was going on.

"I don't see him," I said. "Do you guys?"

The parking lot was in front of the school building. To the left of that was the field where the football and soccer teams practiced, but the field was completely empty.

The sun was so bright overhead that I had to put my hands over my eyes to see. I could feel sweat already beading up on the tip of my nose from how hot it was.

"Nothing," Bloom said, jogging down to the side of the school to see more of the grassy field. "Nothing back here either."

"*Mochi!*" Patrick shouted, cupping his hands over his mouth. "*Mochiiiiii!*"

Nothing answered except for a few birds that got spooked. They fluttered in some trees next to us and then flew away over the school.

I leaned over and rested my hands on my knees as I caught my breath, staring at the side of the school. There were scorch marks left behind whenever the tele-pins were used, but I couldn't see anything that looked like that in the grass.

Bloom was jogging back to us when she slipped, throwing her arms out, but catching herself just before landing on the ground.

"You okay?" Patrick said, squinting his eyes to see farther out.

"Shut up," she said playfully, and then pointed at him. "Look at me! My jeans are ruined because I got some kind of fruit mush all over them back in your office, but I didn't wanna say anything since, y'know, you were all tears back there."

Patrick looked at the back of Bloom's leg as she posed. "Oh, that's my apple basket."

I remembered the basket that Bloom was talking about. I almost knocked it over when I first met Patrick earlier that day. Plus, I remembered all the super gross tiny flies around it.

"Uh, yeah," Bloom said. "I know. A whole basket fulla *rotten* apples."

"Sorry 'bout that," Patrick said.

"Maybe eat them before they go bad?" Bloom suggested, scraping off parts of her jeans where the apple mush was thicker.

"Oh, I don't eat them," Patrick said. "I'm allergic to apples."

Bloom and I looked at each other, confused.

"Then why do you have so many?" I asked.

"That's what I was using to test the tele-pins," Patrick explained.

"Wait, what?" Bloom said.

"I use apples to test the pins," Patrick repeated. "I still don't know where anything ends up, but at least I know what to look for."

"Ew," I said. "You'd be looking for a huge pile of rotten apples. I'd rather smell a skunk's butt than rotten apples."

Bloom gagged with her tongue out. "*What?*"

I held my hands in front of me like I was surrendering. "Alright, alright, I wouldn't rather smell a skunk's butt. It's just a saying."

"Uhhhh," Bloom let out a laugh. "Pretty sure you're the only one sayin' it, duder."

"Whatever!" I said, a little frustrated, but more embarrassed. "Let's just get back to this! Rotten apples, right? We're looking for a pile of…"

That's when something clicked in my head. It was like a puzzle piece had slipped perfectly into place.

"…rotten apples," I whispered with my jaw dropped. A bit of drool had found its way out of my mouth and headed south on my chin.

Bloom and Patrick stared like something was wrong with me.

I wiped the drool from my mouth. "A rotten apple fell on my head this morning!" I said as I walked to the bike rack.

"I, uh, *heroically* bailed from a stunt and landed against the wall outside Principal Green's office! Oh! Her window was also streaked with apple guts!"

"Apple guts," Bloom repeated. "Nice."

"Right? Zombie caterpillars eating apple guts," I said. "I'm totes makin' a comic outta this, but first... follow me!" I said, running to the principal's window.

I slowed as I got closer. I knew we were on the right track because the air smelled of apples. Kinda reminded me of winter around my house.

I tried to find any signs of the SPUDs or Beck or even Mochi anywhere, but there were none.

"Ew," Bloom said as she got closer. "Look at Principal Green's window. So nasty."

Buchanan School was three stories tall, but that was only on one side of the school. The rest of the school didn't have any rooms above them so they were only one story high. I think the roof was about sixteen feet off the ground.

I glanced at the window and saw how the dried apple guts had dripped from the top to the bottom. The brick walls above the window were also stained. The trail of mushed apples went all the way up the side of the building until...

"There!" Patrick said, pointing at the roof.

It was only an instant, but I saw the same thing Patrick did – the very tip of a SPUD's foot that pulled away from the edge of the roof.

"Gotcha," I whispered.

"How're you gonna get up there?" Bloom asked.

I was hoping the answer would be obvious, like there was gonna be a ladder going up the side of the building somewhere nearby, but that wasn't the case.

I turned around, looking at the bike rack behind us. Among the several dozen bikes that were locked up, mine was right in the middle. The thrusters Beck had built were still tied to the sides.

And then I remembered that Beck said there was enough air left in the thrusters for one more jump.

"You guys," I said. "I've got a stupid idea."

34

Outside. 1:17 PM.
Three minutes until Mochi reboots.

I unlocked my bike and pulled it away from the rack.

"Are you nuts? This *is* stupid!" Bloom said, following me as I ran the bike back about ten feet. "Do you remember what happened this morning?"

...déjà vu...

"Uh, yeah," I said. "I was there, y'know."

"Okay, then you remember crashing into the wall of bricks over there," Bloom said. "Because for a second I thought you forgot just how dangerous this was."

"Oh, it's a lot more dangerous than that," I said. "This morning, all I wanted to do was jump over the bike rack. This time, I'm gonna try ramping up to the roof."

"When you say it out loud like that," Bloom said. "It sounds like you've lost your marbles. Just... are you sure about this?"

"Of course!" I said, puffing out my chest. "It'll be easy. I've done this stunt a million times in my dreams. I only chickened out this morning because I thought I was gonna die."

"You're being way too honest right now. Are you sure you haven't gone crazy?"

My only answer was a smile.

I looked at the roof of the school. Beck and the other SPUDs were nowhere to be seen, but I knew they were up there. That meant Mochi was up there too.

"Beck made these thrusters for me," I said, tapping at one of them with the bottom of my shoe. "He said if I gave it full power I'd end up jumping over the school. They have enough air left for one good jump."

"Don't jump over the school!" Patrick said. "Just jump on *top* of it."

"What do I do to Mochi when I get up there?" I asked Patrick. "I mean, if I don't die."

"Mochi has the same switch under the inside of the back of his head," Patrick said. "All you have to do is slide it over. It'll be stiff, so you'll have to push really hard."

"Anything else after that?" I asked, taking a seat on my bike.

Patrick paused. "No. He should switch on just fine. I'll go back to my room in the library and monitor him from my computer. Keep your Holo Pen behind your ear so I can talk to you."

I tapped at the back of the Holo Pen, making sure it was still there.

"If you have any problems," Patrick said over his shoulder as he ran back to the front of the school. "Talk to me!"

164

Taking a deep breath, I stared at the top of the roof and gripped the handlebars of my bike, listening to the sound of the tightening rubber in my hands. It sounded the same as that morning.

"Max, wait," Bloom said, running up to me.

"There's not much time," I said. "Mochi's only got, like, three minutes left."

"Longest three minutes ever, right?" she asked.

I laughed nervously.

And then Bloom pulled a black piece of cloth out of the back pocket of her jeans. It looked damp from where she had slipped on the rotten apples.

As she unfolded the black fabric, she smiled softly at me. "I took this out of the garbage can," she said. "I thought you'd regret throwing it away."

It was the mask that my great-great-grandad left for me. The one we joked might've been a bank robber's mask. Turns out… it *was* a *ninja* mask.

"Sorry about the apple mush," she said, waving the fabric to air it out.

I kept still as she pulled the mask over my head and down on my face. Not only did it smell like it was a hundred years old, but now it stunk of rotten apples.

Bloom laughed when she got a good look at me wearing the ninja mask. I had accidentally ripped the bottom half off of it when I tried it on earlier so the fabric only covered my head from my eyes up.

"Do I look as silly as I think I do?" I asked.

"Um," she said. "Yup."

She held up her bionic arm so I could see my refection in the metal.

"I look like a pirate!" I said.

"Pirate Max Cooper," Bloom boomed proudly. "So awesome."

"Right?" I asked. "Who doesn't love pirates? I bet Chase *loved* pirates."

"Here," Bloom said, pinching the fabric on the top of my head. And then with the quick jerk of her hand, she ripped the top half of the mask off, leaving the fabric that only covered my eyes. "Much better."

The fabric pushed down around my ears, making them stick out a bit. Maybe that was a good thing though, y'know, for secret identities and stuff.

I took a deep breath, gripping my handlebars again. I knew what I had to do. I had to crank the thrusters as high as they could go, and then nail the lip at the bike rack. It probably wasn't even going to be that hard, but for some reason I was finding it impossible to move.

"What're you waiting for?" Bloom said after backing away a few feet.

"Nothing," I said, feeling the exact same thing I had felt that morning.

Fear. And I was drowning in it.

I bailed the first time I tried the stunt. What if I bailed a second time?

No.

I couldn't think like that.

Mochi was still up there, and I had a shot at saving him.

I had to go through with it.

Clenching my jaw, I reached down and cranked the knob on the thrusters as far as they could go. I had ten seconds until they went off.

Probably ten of the longest seconds of my life.

Actually, no. For some reason, the thrusters fired the second I touched my handlebars again, and I was off. Probably a good thing because it meant I didn't have time to think about what I was doing.

Wouldn't have mattered anyway because my bike was completely *out* of my control. It was going so fast that I couldn't have steered it if I wanted to.

In fact, the only thing I was able to do was scream at the top of my lungs.

35

Outside. 1:18 PM.
Two minutes until Mochi reboots.

When you're in the air, floating through clouds, nothing can hurt you. You're as free as a bird, drifting aimlessly as the wind sifts through the hairs on your arms and legs.

You're not tethered to the Earth by the invisible villain known as gravity.

And it was in that moment that I realized how two-dimensional my world had been. I was like a square that had somehow become a cube.

The sky was above me. The clouds were right next to me. And the roof of the school was below me.

Yep. I had graduated from humanity and become one with time and space, seeing the past and the present and the future all at once. And seeing that roof underneath me again, but a little closer.

All the SPUDs were gathered in a little cluster. Beck was several feet away looking at the letter. Mochi was laying on his face. And that roof… that roof was getting closer and closer…

OMG, that roof was getting closer and closer!

I panicked, suddenly realizing I was still flying through the air on the seat of my bike. When I hit the lip, I was so afraid that I zoned out.

"Zone back in, zone back in!" I repeated. "*Zone back in!*"

I wasn't sure how I was going to land, but then realized it didn't matter what I *wanted* to do. My bike had drifted far enough away from me that my body was gonna slam into the rooftop.

Awesome. I was gonna have to use my body to break my fall. Or the fall was going to break my body. One of those two.

Good times.

My bike crashed first on the roof, bucking wildly like an out-of-control horse. It actually worked out because it smashed into a couple of SPUDs, sending their little robot body parts flying off the edge of the building.

I landed *hard* on the roof.

Man, I didn't even, like, roll across the roof or tumble until I stopped. My body was just, like, *PLOP*. It even made that sound.

I turned over so I could see the sky, and then I lifted my fist into the air. "…*Naaaaaailed it*."

The SPUDs were clustered in a group and didn't move from their spot. Beck probably needed to give them the command to attack.

"Keep it down!" Beck said, but didn't turn around. He must've thought the SPUDs were having a dance party or something because there was *no way* he didn't hear me crash.

When I glanced over at my ex-bestie, his back was to me. Underneath one of his spider legs was the letter. He was too distracted by it to even *look* at anything else in the world, like when I zone out playing video games.

Nearly ten feet away from me was Mochi, laying face first in the small pebbles on the rooftop. I had to get to him before Beck saw me. All I needed to do was flip the switch Patrick told me about and Mochi would be fine. Hopefully.

The Holo Pen behind my ear vibrated. Through the tiny speaker on the side of the pen, the computer spoke only loudly enough so only I could hear it. "*Incoming call from Patrick Scott... Incoming call from Patrick Scott...*"

I carefully tapped the butt of my pen to answer it. "Uh, hello?" I whispered.

"Max, can you hear me?" Patrick said over the Holo Pen.

I watched Beck as I whispered, wondering if Squids had superhearing or not. "Loud and clear," I said, trying to sound like a cool secret agent on a mission. "I see the package, repeat, I see the package."

"What package? I thought you were going to the roof! Are you at the mailbox or something?"

There wasn't enough time to explain cool agent phrases. "I see Mochi," I whispered. "He's on his face about ten feet away."

"Then what're you waiting for?"

"I'd probably be done by now if I didn't have to answer a phone call!" I said way too loudly.

Beck's little spider legs jabbed at the floor as he turned around. "We're gonna get caught if you SPUDs don't pipe down!" he said, still looking down at the letter. When he looked up at me, he froze.

So did I.

The two of us stared at each other at eye level since I was on my belly and he was without his Tenderfoot Shell. I think he was weirded out by the fact that I was wearing a ninja mask though.

"This letter has nothing else to decode!" Beck erupted. "It's just a folded sheet of paper that has a bunch of garbage drawings and *one* code! You *lied* to me!"

Beck poked a hole in the letter and whipped it through the air like a playing card.

I flinched, feeling the sharp corner hit me on my cheek.

"Why did you lie to me?" Beck shouted angrily.

"I wasn't lying!" I said, feeling stupid. "I mean, yes, I *kind* of was, but—"

"You said it was *filled* with coded messages and secrets!"

"Well, it's not!" I said. "I only told you that because you were so stoked about it! I made a mistake, but that doesn't give you the right to do all the things you did!"

"You didn't give me any choice!" Beck screamed inside his mask.

"Oh, you were *forced* to reprogram the SPUDs?" I said. "You were *forced* to kidnap Mochi? You were *forced* to steal that letter from me?"

Beck didn't even hesitate, which was how I knew he was too far-gone. "Yes!" he screamed at me.

My brain was a bonfire of anger as I pulled the monocle from my pocket. I picked up the letter off the ground and held the two of them together, waving them both at my ex-best friend. "Well, there's no more secret codes or messages or—"

I stopped in my tracks, staring at the monocle I was holding against my great-great-grandad's letter. Through the glass I saw a single word that I couldn't see before: WAR.

There *was* a message on the letter. It was written with invisible ink and the monocle was the way of seeing it!

"Huh," I grunted, and then stupidly said out loud, "Wouldja lookit that? There *is* another secret note. We just needed this monocle to read it..."

Beck had his crazy eyes on when I looked back at him. *"Give me that monocle!"*

I wished I had a cool one liner to dish out at him, but I didn't. Instead, I said, "No, thank you!"

Beck raised one of his spider legs and tapped at it with another one of his legs. I heard the same beeping sound I had heard back in the library before being attacked. He was giving the SPUDs a command. "Get him!" he growled.

The clustered SPUDs across the rooftop came to life, turning their red eyes on me. And then altogether, they scampered at me.

"Mochi!" Patrick shouted through my Holo Pen. "Get Mochi!"

Clutching the letter and monocle in my hand, I spun around and took off like a bat outta heck, kicking up small pebbles and rocks each time my foot clapped against the ground. Mochi was close so it took almost no time for me to get to him, but it also meant that Beck's SPUDs would be there at any moment.

The faint sound of sirens filled the air. They were far off, but they were getting closer. Lexi must've had Principal Green call the police.

Dropping to my thigh, I slid on the pebbles, scooping Mochi's lifeless body into my arms. I pushed my finger into the spot that Patrick had told me about. Mochi's face was a black screen as his arms and legs dangled underneath him.

"Where is it?" I said. "Where's the 'on' button?"

Patrick's voice came through my Holo Pen. "It's that spot at the base of his neck!"

When I wiggled my finger, I could feel what Patrick was talking about. It was a tiny little switch that was slid all the way to the left. I used my finger, pressing hard against it until it slid back to the right.

"*SCHICK!*"

Nothing happened.

"Um… what?" I said, flipping the switch back and forth. "Patrick, nothing's happening!"

"*SCHICK, SCHICK! SCHICK, SCHICK!*"

"What do you mean nothing's happening?" Patrick's voice sounded frantic.

"I'm switching him on and off," I said. "Beck must've hurt him more than we thought!"

"Max!" Patrick said. "You gotta switch him on! He's been off for too long!"

"I'm trying!" I said, frustrated and scared. I was outta ideas, so I clenched my jaw and slammed my fist down on the broken SPUD.

CLUNK!

Suddenly the screen on Mochi's face lit up and then flickered like an old television set.

"*There!*" Patrick said. "He's coming online! I can see him on my computer... but... oh-noes..."

Mochi's face flashed once more, and then went black except for a message in green text at the center of the screen.

"*SYSTEM REBOOTING. 77% complete. Please do not switch SPUD off until completely rebooted. Thank you. – Tenderfoot Industries.*"

I was too late.

36

I stared at Mochi's face as Beck's SPUDs grew closer. I could hear the pitter patter of robotic feet crunching across the pebbled rooftop.

"No…" Patrick's voice whispered.
My heart sunk.
It was literally the worst day of my life.
Mochi was the only thing that could've been saved, and I completely bombed it. Mochi's body was coming back online, but Mochi was gone. In just a few short seconds, the SPUD in my arms would turn back on and probably join his little SPUD brothers in attacking me.

175

"SYSTEM REBOOTING. 89% complete. Please do not switch SPUD off until completely rebooted. Thank you. – Tenderfoot Industries."

On the Holo Pen, I could hear Patrick furiously typing into his computer as he whispered. *"Come on, come on, come on..."*

Beck's SPUDs were coming at full speed. I should've gotten up, but I didn't want to let Mochi go. He was just a robot, but for some reason I wanted to hold him and hug him back to life.

"Max, I have an idea!" Patrick shouted. "But you gotta switch him off, like, *right now!* Before that reboot reaches a hundred percent!"

I looked at the message on Mochi's face.

"SYSTEM REBOOTING. 98% complete. Please do not switch SPUD off until completely rebooted. Thank you. – Tenderfoot Industries."

"Hurry!" Patrick screamed.

My finger found the switch again, and I slid it back to the left.

Mochi's face made a *"BLIP BLIP"* sound and went back to a black screen.

"Should I switch it back now?" I asked.

"No," Patrick said. "I connected to him using my computer so all that needs to happen is..." I heard a single click over the Holo Pen.

At that very instant, Beck's SPUDs swarmed me like robotic insects. They peeled Mochi away from my hands and tried pulling me down to the floor.

The letter and monocle were still in my right hand. I held them high over my head trying to keep them safe.

I twirled, freaking out, trying to shake the SPUDs off, but it wasn't working. They pinched at my clothing, keeping me from barely moving. The harder I tried, the more frozen I felt. The whole thing was like a fever dream.

Beck was standing back laughing. "Shoulda just given me what I wanted, bro!"

My right arm was still high over my head, but my left was trapped at my side. Somehow, I managed to free that arm and clutched at the back of one of the SPUDs, peeling him off my body.

I twirled again, tossing him across the roof as hard as I could, hoping his body would bust apart when he hit the ground, but I wasn't strong enough. The SPUD flipped in the air and landed on his hands and feet like a cat.

My mind was racing. SPUDs were climbing my body. The letter and the monocle were going to be Beck's soon enough.

But there was no way I was going to give up without a fight.

It was a struggle to stay standing, but I managed to do it. Kicking my feet wildly, I shook a couple of SPUDs off. When they landed on the floor, I soccer punted them across the rooftop, hard enough that the magnets keeping them together failed, sending robot parts across the roof.

That only seemed to anger the other SPUDs trying to take me down. One of the SPUDs even started pulling my hair!

I tried to keep my feet firmly planted on the rooftop. The only thing I wanted to do was keep from falling over, but I knew I was only a few seconds away from doing just that.

And that's when it happened. I felt something jump on my shoulders and yank the SPUD off my head.

The other SPUDs stopped what they were doing to look at the thing above them.

It was Mochi with his big green eyes and a smile on his screen.

"Hi!" Mochi chimed as if the worst thing in the world wasn't happening to me. "My favorite thing ever is *caramel pizza*! *What's yours?*"

Patrick's voice was back, but not in the Holo Pen behind my ear. A small screen popped up in the corner of Mochi's face that had a video feed of Patrick working in his office. "You did it!" he said. "You killed the reboot just in time! He's still mostly himself! *Mostly.*"

"Great," I said, feeling Beck's SPUDs start to move again. "But can we talk details later? Is there any way Mochi can help me right now?"

"Oh, wow," Patrick said. "Yeah, that's bad. I can see them through the camera on Mochi's head."

I watched Patrick's fingers jab at his keyboard as he stuck his tongue out of the side of his mouth.

"Mochi's not connected to the mainframe," Patrick said. "But he *is* connected to my computer now, which means…" he

177

stopped talking and typed in a bunch of other stuff. "I can upload anything I want into Mochi's brain. Check this out."

Patrick struck his keyboard with one finger.

At the same time, Mochi's body flinched as his green eyes grew huge. And then he looked at me with his serious face. "I know kung-fu…"

In a blur of silver and green, Mochi flipped backward off my head and landed on the ground. He jumped, spinning in a circle with his foot sticking out, helicopter kicking two of Beck's SPUDs off of me.

The other SPUDs dropped to the ground, turning on Mochi rather than me.

Mochi landed perfectly in front of them, huddled in a kung-fu stance. With his tiny robot fingers, he waved, inviting them to come after him.

One by one, Beck's SPUDs dashed at Mochi, and one by one, Mochi completely wrecked them with kung-fu moves. Spinning leg kicks, fierce uppercuts, and an occasional head-butt.

All I had to do was sit back and watch Mochi take care of business. Robots fighting other robots was seriously pretty sweet.

It was down to Mochi and one last SPUD. Both robots circled each other, Mochi with his hand out and the other SPUD with his fists up.

"Why are we even fighting?" the SPUD asked. "Are we not… brothers?"

Mochi cocked an eyebrow on his screen, surprised by the sudden question.

"Did that SPUD just ask if they were brothers?" Patrick asked incredulously through my Holo Pen.

The SPUD threw his fist. Mochi easily caught it with his open hand, and then swung his other arm underneath the SPUD, lifting him into the air.

But before Mochi could toss the SPUD aside, Beck appeared out of nowhere, wrapping his spider legs around both of the SPUDs. Mochi tried to free himself, but Beck whipped around, tossing both Mochi and the other SPUD right off the side of the roof.

"No!" I shouted, reaching my hand out, like that was gonna do anything.

"Enough of this!" Beck barked. "If ya want somethin' done right, ya gotta do it yourself!"

I stumbled back, but caught myself from falling over. The letter and the monocle were still in my hand.

"Give them to me!" Beck said, inching forward.

Mochi was gone.

The other SPUDs were in pieces across the rooftop.

Beck and I were the only two left.

It was our showdown.

37

Beck continued to move slowly in my direction. The edge of the roof behind me was about five or six feet away, so I wasn't about to back up any farther

The police sirens were getting louder, but they still weren't at the school.

I was fed up. The weight of everything that happened that day finally crushed me, and I shouted, "*What the heck's your problem?*"

The squid in the helmet stopped. "Max," Beck finally sighed, suddenly super chill. Like, *creepy* chill. "You've been a good… '*friend*' isn't the right word… you've been a good *human* to me."

My lungs felt like they had gotten the wind sucked out of them. When I finally took a breath, I spoke. "That's *all* I was to you? Just a *human?*"

Beck raised the spot above his eyes where eyebrows would be if he had them. "Sorry, dude. It's not *you*… it's *me*. I've just never felt a real connection to anyone in the human race."

I couldn't believe what I was hearing. I thought I was *losing* my best friend. As it turned out, he was *never* my best friend.

"And I'm just so *bored* with *everything*," Beck went on. "I've played by Buchanan's rules for too long, but I'm *done* playing by the rules. I *learned* something today, you know."

"Yeah? What's that?"

Beck paused, giving me the evil squid eye. "I learned that waiting around for *something* to happen means that *nothing* will ever happen. We're all in charge of our own *fate* –

our own *legacy* – and if we want something more from life…
we have to go and *get* it."

I blinked. This *was* a villain's origin story. I was just
wrong about *who* the villain was.

"You sound like some kind of psycho," I said. It was so
ridiculous that I couldn't help but chuckle. Beck really *was*
some kind of nut.

But Beck wasn't playing nice anymore. "I am *not* a
psycho! I'm *enlightened!*"

"Yup! That's exactly what a psycho would say!"

"I'm *awake*, Max! And I'm gonna wake everyone else
up too!" Beck screamed like a banshee. "Give me the
monocle!"

I was so filled with rage that I spoke without thinking.
"Come and get it!"

Beck went "full crazy" and ran toward me. His spider
legs were moving so fast that I couldn't even see them.

"That was a mistake," I muttered to myself.

I took a step backward, aware that the edge of the
building was still about five feet behind me. For the rest of my

life, I knew I was going to have nightmares of that exact moment. That was, if I survived.

Beck let out one last battle cry as he shot off the ground. As he flew at me, he angled his helmet so it would hit me with the top of the glass. That dude was gonna head-butt me!

The ninja mask was making it hard to see anything so I yanked it off my face.

"Give me what's mine!" Beck shrieked.

I gasped, raising my hands in the air, expecting a new kind of pain I had never felt before – a pain *so epic* that even the planet would flinch and be like, "Oh, man!"

But… it never happened.

My eye were squeezed shut so tight that all I saw were the red vessels behind my eyelids. I couldn't shut my ears though and heard the whirring sounds of Beck's spider legs going crazy.

I wasn't sure what was happening. Was I dead and floating over my lifeless body? Was that why I felt no pain?

I opened my eyes slightly, afraid of what I was about to see.

There, in front of me, was Beck. His helmet was facing me and his eyes were still filled with fury, staring me down. His spider legs were moving frantically in the air behind him.

But he wasn't moving.

I LOL'd when I realized I was *holding* him. I *caught* him in my hands when he jumped at me. He was completely helpless!

At that moment, the door across the rooftop burst open, shattering at the hinges.

Bloom came running out with Lexi right behind her. They both skidded to a stop when they saw me carrying Beck, and their jaws dropped when they saw the mess of SPUD parts scattered across their path.

Principal Green stepped out from the broken door too. "Seriously? You could've just turned the doorknob, Bloom. Just because you have a bionic arm doesn't mean you need to break doors down."

"Max was in trouble!" Bloom said. "I got caught up in the moment!"

Off the edge of the building, I watched as several police cars pulled into Buchanan's parking lot. Beck swirled around in his helmet until he was looking at the squad cars too.

"Those are for me?" Beck wheezed, frightened. His little squid body scrunched up, and then his helmet filled with black ink. "Aw, *dang it!*"

That was it – Beck had ink'd himself, which meant he couldn't see or do anything until his water was switched out.

I sighed, relieved that the battle was over.

38

I was still on the roof, sitting a few feet away from the edge of the school building watching the police in the parking lot as they talked to Beck. One of the officers had given me a blanket that I had draped over my shoulders even though it was hot and muggy out. I don't know – for some reason it felt like I should wear it.

Because of all the commotion, a lot of the students from the school had come out to see what all the fuss was about. It was the most excitement anyone had seen all year.

Bloom scooted next to me on the floor of the roof. "Spicy day, huh?"

I nodded, then suddenly remembered that Mochi was thrown from the building.

"Wait," I said, feeling a knot in my stomach. "Where's Mochi? Beck got ahold of him and threw him—"

"He's fine!" Patrick said from behind me.

When I turned, I saw Patrick and Lexi with Mochi walking alongside them. Patrick had my bike and was guiding it by just the seat.

"He landed in the grass!" Lexi said, waving to me. "When I was in Principal Green's office telling her about Beck and his mind-controlled SPUDs, I saw Mochi drop off the side. I ran and got him. And then Patrick took him before I came up here with Bloom."

Mochi stood at attention, saluting. "Pleasure to work with you today, sir," he said sternly. "Permission to dance? I'm especially good at the 'robot.'"

"No," Patrick hissed. "Keep it down, Mochi. The principal's coming!"

Principal Green cleared her throat as she approached us. She took a deep breath and shook her head as she watched the police put Beck in a squad car and close the door.

"What's gonna happen to him?" I asked.

"Beck? Oh, he's in *alotta* trouble," the principal said. "I'm not exactly sure though. Beck's the first Tenderfoot Squid to ever act out like this… *ever*. The folks at Tenderfoot Industries said they want to talk to him about it first. After that, we might not see him again."

I was sad to hear that.

"Or he might be back in a week," Principal Green added. "For what he did, I'd only give him a week in detention."

"That's it?" I said. "A *week* in The Freezer?"

The principal eyeballed me. She looked angry, but in a playful way. "*You* should be more worried about yourself, Mr. Cooper. Your Holo Pen says you haven't been in *any* of your classes today!"

I scratched the back of my neck. "You said I could skip so I could decode my time capsule letter."

"I said you could skip the remainder of *one* class!" Principal Green huffed. "Not *all* your classes!"

I laughed, uncomfortable. "Hehe, um… my bad."

"Mm-hmm," Principal Green hummed. "We'll figure out how to handle that after everything's calmed down out here."

Patrick snorted a laugh.

Principal Green turned to him, changing the subject. "And you… Beck said he was using a teleporter that *you created.* Is this true?"

Patrick stared at the floor. "Uh, yeah," he said, flustered. "I'm sorry about the apples on your window. I was gonna tell you about it when it was finished, but—"

"Don't apologize!" the principal laughed. "What you did is a *big deal!* A big enough deal that when the people of Tenderfoot Industries come and talk to Beck, they're going to take a look at your teleporter too!" Principal Green shrugged. "They'll *probably* take it *away*, but this could mean big things for you."

Mochi's face lit up with a smile.

Principal Green raised one eyebrow and looked at the SPUD suspiciously.

My friends and I held our breath, worried that Mochi had given himself away. Sure, he was harmless, but if Tenderfoot Industries knew about Mochi, they'd probably want to take him away too.

Mochi continued to smile at the principal, but said nothing.

"Anything else you'd like to tell me, Patrick?" Principal Green asked, not breaking eye contact with the smiling SPUD.

Patrick fumbled over some sounds.

After all the work it took to make sure Mochi was safe, I couldn't just let Principal Green hand him over to Tenderfoot Industries.

"Nope!" I said quickly, cutting Patrick off from accidentally saying too much. "We're good. Nothing else to say over here, sir. Er, I mean, ma'am."

The principal put her hands behind her back and raised her nose at Mochi. "Alright then," she said. "The SPUDs will be getting their systems completely reset after school tonight. Tenderfoot Industries employees will personally see to it that *every* SPUD is included."

Patrick winced.

"I suggest you take *your* SPUD home with you tonight," the principal said over her shoulder as she walked away.

"Whoa," Bloom said, watching the principal walk away. "Do you think she knows?"

"She totally knows," Lexi said.

"Thanks, man," Patrick said. My bike was still by his side.

I pointed at the thrusters Beck had made. "What d'you think?" I asked.

Patrick smiled and shrugged his shoulder. "Eh, it's clever, but *amateur*. I can set you up with something *a lot* better next time."

"Next time, huh?"

Patrick looked down and nodded his head at the schoolyard full of kids.

Everyone was talking and laughing with each other in a way I had never seen before. Many were just happy to be out of their classrooms, but there were a few of them who were interested in what had happened on the roof, watching carefully like they were studying or something.

A flash caught my eye. It was the tinfoil hat on top of Nunchuck Chuck's head. He actually wasn't shouting anything about a conspiracy theory. He was just staring up at my friends and me.

"I think you started something today," Patrick said. "You opened Pandora's box."

"Pandora's what now?" I said.

"It's from Greek mythology," Patrick explained. "Pandora was a woman who had a box that was never supposed to be opened. Well, she opened it, and out of the box came all sorts of evil things. Pandora tried to get them back into the box, but it was too late… they all got out."

"Bummer," I said.

"You opened that box," Patrick continued. "After everyone hears about this epic adventure, they'll want the same thing – well, not everybody, but enough to cause headaches. The crazies are gonna come out to play, and when they do, you'll need all the help you can get."

"You're saying you'll help me?"

"You saved my best friend," Patrick said, patting Mochi on the head. "I owe you."

Patrick took Mochi in his arms and walked to the doors that led back into the school. Principal Green moved her arms in the air, speaking into the Holo Pen behind her head. Lexi and Bloom were still right by my side.

I took the monocle and the letter out from my front pocket. Pressing the monocle against my eye, I looked at the spot on the letter I had seen earlier – the spot that had *WAR* written on it in invisible ink.

"What're you doing?" Lexi asked.

"There's another message on this letter that you can only see with this monocle," I said.

"No way!" Bloom said. "What's it say?"

I thought the message was going to say something about a *war*, but it turns out that I only saw a small part of the message earlier. The actual message said something completely different.

In big ol' capital letters, Great-Great-Grandpa Chase Cooper had written, "BEWARE OF THE SCAVENGERS."

"What's that mean?" Bloom asked. "Who are The Scavengers?"

The message sent a chill down my spine. The whispers I had heard in the dungeon, they had said something about The Scavengers. It was too much of a coincidence for me to ignore.

But I didn't tell Bloom or Lexi any of that. There was no need to get them worried. "Beats me," I said. "Prob'ly nothing to worry about."

The three of us sat on the rooftop of the school. Principal Green would shout at us to get back to class soon, but for the next few minutes, we were okay to watch the clouds together.

The adventure was over – the one that my great-great-grandfather Chase Cooper had started over a hundred years ago. It was crazy to think that a simple letter he left could cause so much trouble in the future.

Well, it was the future for him. And at that point in the day, it was the past for me.

A cloud drifted in front of the sun, casting a shadow across the school parking lot. I watched as the shadow glided over each car until it finally shrouded us on the roof.

The air sifted through the hairs on my arm, giving me goose bumps, and then it occurred to me...

The adventure *wasn't* over. It was just beginning.

Patrick was right. Life was about to get much, *much* crazier now that the box had been opened.

The whispers – the message about The Scavengers – the big metal door in the dungeon – those were questions that I *needed* answers for.

I reached my hand back and felt the ninja mask I had stuffed in my back pocket after giving Beck to the police.

The mask had become more than a piece of dirty old fabric. It had become a sign of courage. A sign of strength. Hope. It was the light in my dark world. It had become all these things to me, and I decided right there that I wanted it to be the same for the rest of the students at Buchanan School in the year 2099.

It was my past, my present, and my future.

It was going to be my legacy.

My name is Max Cooper... and I'm a middle school ninja.

The Middle School Ninja will return.

Dun dun dunnnnnn…

Oh, the life of being a ninja. I know what you're thinking – it's an awesome life filled with secrets, crazy ninja moves, and running on the tops of trees. Well, you're right. I'm not gonna lie to you – it's an absolutely *fantastic* life.

But it wasn't always that way.

This might surprise you, but ninjas are often seen as the *bad* guys. I know, right? I had no idea either until I became one. Though looking back, I should've seen the signs early on. You know what they say – hindsight is 20/20.

So this is my story – my diary…er, my *chronicle*. I feel as though it has to be told for others to read so they can learn about the events at Buchanan School. History has to be studied and learned from or else it's destined to repeat itself. And that's something I cannot allow.

My name is Chase Cooper, and I'm eleven years old.

I'm the kind of kid that likes to read comic books and watch old horror movies with my dad. If you were to see me walking down the street, you'd try your best not to bump into me, but only because I'm sorta scrawny. I see all these articles online with titles about losing weight and getting rid of unwanted body fat, and my jaw just drops because I can't gain weight to save my life! I've started working out with my dad when he gets home from work, but it's hard to keep up with him.

All this to say that if you saw me, the last thing you'd think was "dangerous ninja."

I'm not the most popular kid in school, that's for sure. I've never had a girlfriend, and I've never played sports outside of gym class. That's not true – I was on a soccer team in third grade, but after a shin guard to the face and a broken nose, I quit.

So I'm scrawny and unpopular. What else can I apply to those two traits for a completely wretched experience? The *start* of school. But wait! Let's multiply that by a million – I'm also the *new* kid at this particular school.

My parents decided to move across town over the summer so we could live in a slightly larger house. I mean, really? How selfish is *that*? A bigger house, but social death for me! Being in a new district means an entire herd of new students that I don't know.

Well, that's not entirely true either. I know Zoe. She's the same age as me, but doesn't really count because she's my cousin.

Luckily, we had the same gym class together. She was surprised to see me on that first day. I remember it well – it was a Monday, and the day I caught my first glimpse of the ninjas at Buchanan.

"Chase?" Zoe asked. She was wearing gym shorts and a tank top with the school's mascot on it.

"Hey, Zoe," I said.

She looked surprised. "It *is* you! What're you doing *here*?"

Going to school, dummy. That's what I *wanted* to say, but decided against it. "My parents moved to this side of town so I go to school here now."

Zoe laughed. "That's so cool! My own cousin in the same school as me! What fun we'll have!"

I looked at her silky hair and perfect skin. She kind of looked like one of those models on teenybopper magazines. Yeah, there was no way she'd keep herself affiliated with the likes of me, but I gave her the benefit of the doubt. "Uh-huh, it'll be great," I sighed.

The coach, Mr. Cooper, was at the front of the gymnasium checking off students he knew. He walked up to the rest and asked for their names and grade. Finally, he approached Zoe and me.

"Good morning, Zoe," Mr. Cooper said as he scraped a checkmark into the attendance list. Then he looked at me. "And what's your name?"

Zoe answered for me. "This is Chase Cooper. He's my cousin," she said with a smile.

"Good to have you here," said Mr. Cooper. Then he pointed at Zoe. "She's a good kid to have as a cousin. It's the start of school, but I've already seen her on several try-out lists. You'll do good to follow her lead."

I faked a smile. "Sure."

As Mr. Cooper walked away, Zoe continued speaking. "Why didn't you tell me you were starting at this school?"

I shrugged my shoulders. "We don't really talk that much, and it never came up in conversation. We hardly ever see each other."

Zoe crinkled her nose. "We see each other *every weekend*. Our families have Sunday brunch together at the park!"

I couldn't argue with her. "It's just a little embarrassing."

"You have nothing to be embarrassed about. Starting a new school might be weird, but it's not like you have the ability to control a situation like that," she said.

I didn't want to tell her I was embarrassed and scared of being the new kid. That making friends isn't a strength of mine, and I'm destined to be that kid who walks swiftly through the hallways, clutching my backpack straps and staring at the floor, hoping I don't make eye contact with someone with anger management issues. So I didn't say any of that. "You're right. I think it's just the first day jitters, y'know?"

Zoe's eyes sparkled. She didn't have a clue. "Welcome to the club. We've *all* got the first day jitters. My dad always says the pool is coldest when you first touch the water so the best thing to do is dive right in."

I wasn't sure what my cousin was trying to say. So I replied with, "Wise words."

Zoe looked off to her left and noticed a boy standing alone. "That's Wyatt. He's never really talked to anyone here. He keeps to himself – always has. Which is why he probably doesn't have any friends."

Wyatt was short. He had wavy black hair and a pale complexion that would make a vampire jealous. He kind of looked like a porcelain doll. "Has anyone tried to be *his* friend?"

"Actually, yes. *I* tried talking to him last year, but he wouldn't hear any of it," she sighed. "He was a *jerk* to me."

"Why are you telling me this?" I asked.

Zoe glanced at me. "Because I don't want you to be like him."

I tightened a smile. When I looked back at Wyatt, he was gone.

"So have you raised any money yet for the food drive?" Zoe asked out of nowhere.

"Food drive?" I asked. "I haven't heard of anything about that."

"They sent a pamphlet to all of the student's houses last week," she said. "Oh, that's right… you just moved into your new place, didn't you?"

I nodded.

"Well, it's probably somewhere at your house. We're supposed to raise money by selling fruit or something. I'm already up to ten boxes sold."

"Is there a prize or anything?" I asked. Normally these kinds of things had cool prizes – ray guns and little helicopters and stuff.

"Not a prize for one person, but if the school collectively raises over ten grand, we get to take a trip the week before school is out."

"Where to?"

Zoe shrugged her shoulders. "Does it matter? Anything to get out of school for a day."

I smiled at my cousin. She was actually a little cooler than I thought.

Mr. Cooper opened the side door to the gymnasium. Thank goodness too because Zoe's conversation was making me feel a little edgy. He stepped outside and held the door open with his foot, ushering the rest of us to exit the gym for some "productive activity" outside. Great, just what I needed. Exercise.

Outside, the students were given a few different options. Being the first day of school, Mr. Cooper apparently thought the best thing to do was take it lightly and allow kids to choose what sport they wanted to play. Some played football. Only a couple played basketball. The rest of them, like me, chose to walk laps around the track. It was the easiest option that didn't require choosing teams or working up a sweat.

I could tell Zoe wanted to play football with a few of her friends, but decided to walk the track by my side. It wasn't a huge sacrifice for her, but I appreciated it. A little goes a long way with me.

"So what do you want to know?" she asked.

I didn't understand her question. "What do you mean?"

"About this school. What do you want to know about this school? I imagine most schools are the same, but there's gotta be a *couple* differences here and there. What'd you do at your old school?"

I thought about it for a moment. "I didn't do much. I was in the art club, but that's about it."

"That's fun," Zoe said as she started skipping along the track.

Zoe reminded me of my sister, Lucy, who was also somewhere in the building, adjusting to life as a new student. To be fair, it was far easier for her since she was in third grade. Most third graders barely even know they exist. They haven't become "self aware" yet – like artificial intelligence that hasn't realized it has an identity.

Zoe spoke in an excited manner, which was surprisingly contagious. "There's a *ton* of stuff to do here. Not a lot of schools have as much as us. Buchanan actually prides itself on how huge of a selection we have. There's all kinds of sports teams, different groups, and a bunch of random clubs you can join. I'm sure there's an art club somewhere around here. I'll help you find it."

I nodded my head, but was distracted by some movement out of the corner of my eye. It was the edge of the track where the tree line was the thickest. I stopped in place and stared for a second to see if anything moved again, but nothing did.

"What is it?" Zoe asked.

I kept staring into the dense foliage. It was just a mess of green leaves and heavy shadows - except for a pair of the whitest eyes I'd ever seen. I froze in place and rubbed my eyes. Am I seeing things straight or was it part of the "first day jitters" that Zoe and I spoke about? When I looked again, they were gone.

"I guess I just…" I stopped talking when I looked at Zoe's face.

Zoe was standing behind me with her eyes peeled wide open, staring into the same spot in the tree line that I was studying only seconds ago. "Did you see that?" she asked.

A chill ran down my spine. "I did. Do you know what it was?"

She shook her head and started walking along the track again. "Come on. Let's get out of here. I think I'd rather *not* get eaten by a creature in the woods today."

I knew it wasn't a monster that we had seen. I'm not that into scary stories and watch enough with my dad to know that monsters are fake… at least I *think* they're fake. At that moment, I didn't feel the need to test that theory so I caught up with Zoe and we spent the rest of class making jokes to distract ourselves from whatever it was that had spied on us.

Little did I know that it was the first time I'd ever seen a ninja. I'd do anything to take that moment back and just keep walking. Of course, that's not how it turned out, and my curiosity got the better of me.

From Marcus Emerson:

Stories – what an incredible way to open one's mind to a fantastic world of adventure. It's my hope that this story has inspired you in some way, lighting a fire that maybe you didn't know you had. Keep that flame burning no matter what. It represents your sense of adventure and creativity, and that's something nobody can take from you. Thanks for reading! If you enjoyed this book, I ask that you help spread the word by sharing it or leaving an honest review!

- Marcus
- m@MarcusEmerson.com

35882468R00124

Made in the USA
Middletown, DE
18 October 2016